The Legend of

JIMMY
SPOON

Washakie, Chief of the Eastern Wind River Shoshoni. Courtesy of American Heritage Center, University of Wyoming.

The Legend of

JIMMY SPOON

Kristiana Gregory

SCHOLASTIC INC.
New York Toronto London Auckland Sydney

Copyright © 1990 by Kristiana Gregory.
All rights reserved. Published by Scholastic Inc., 730 Broadway, New York, NY 10003, by arrangement with
Harcourt Brace Jovanovich, Publishers.
Cover illustration by Greg Shed.
Printed in the U.S.A.
ISBN 0-590-46388-8

24 23 22 21 20 19 18   40   3/0

Note

The Legend of Jimmy Spoon is fiction inspired by *Among the Shoshones*, the memoirs of Elijah Nicholas Wilson. The Wyoming town of Wilson, at the southern base of the Tetons, is named for that author.

During the mid-1800s, there were many tribal chiefs in the Utah-Idaho-Wyoming-Montana territories. Among them were Pocatello of the Northwestern Shoshoni, Tendoy of the Northern Lemhi Shoshoni, and Washakie of the Eastern Wind River Shoshoni. Tendoy, one of Washakie's cousins, was a grandson of Sacajawea, the famous "bird woman" who had guided Lewis and Clark's expedition through the Northwest in 1805–1806. Washakie shared leadership chores with Bannock Chief Tahgee during annual buffalo hunts on the Wyoming and Montana plains.

Acknowledgments

With special thanks to my friends: Shoshone-Bannock tribal historian Judge Clyde M. Hall, for reading my manuscript and offering invaluable insight; Kerwin Toane, for long talks about old ways; also interim photo archivist James W. Carlson and research historian Emmett D. Chisum of the American Heritage Center at the University of Wyoming, Laramie. And to Betty Holbrook, the beacon at Pocatello Public Library who first introduced me to Nick Wilson.

Most especially, thanks to my husband, Kip Rutty, whose tolerance of makeshift dinners on our book-cluttered table makes my writing possible. It is to him this book is dedicated.

Let us therefore make every effort
to do what leads to peace
and to mutual edification.

Romans 14:19

1

An Unhappy Birthday

Drums.

Jimmy awoke with a start. His mother was rushing toward the door with baby Annie in her arms. Emma and Frances were hanging on to her apron, crying in panic.

"Jimmy!" she yelled. "Hurry."

No moon lit their way, and there were no torches this time. The warning drum pounded on as women and children ran through the darkness. They crowded into the log schoolhouse in the center of the fortress.

"Shh," the mothers whispered. But the babies still cried. Jimmy was certain one night the arrows would stop them before they made it to safety.

His family was new to Brigham Young's Mormon settlement and every night they went to bed in fear. Would they be killed in their sleep? Or would the terrible sound of the drum wake them in time?

To the settlers' relief, attacks by the Gosiutes eventually became demands for food or supplies, and the walls of the protective fort were taken down, its wood used to build simple houses. The Shoshoni and Bannock tribes migrated north and only appeared for trading.

"It's cheaper to feed an Indian than to fight him," Brigham Young told Jimmy's father. "A few thousand bushels of wheat a year and whatnot should take care of them."

The pioneers Brigham Young had led across the Great Plains in 1847 were now homesteading the parched Utah territory that bordered a great salt lake. Seeds carried on the fourteen-hundred-mile trek in pouches and letter boxes from Nauvoo, Illinois, had been planted immediately, as were the rose cuttings, geranium slips, and seedling trees that had survived.

Brigham Young told his followers that only by thrift, industry, and working as hard as bees would they prosper. Soon orchards were fragrant with cherry, peach, apple, and apricot blossoms. Rows upon rows of fast-growing poplars waved in the wind. Streams flowing from the towering Wasatch Mountains were used to irrigate the land, and before long trees were shading porches along broad avenues. The Mormon colony flourished at such an amazing pace that it was to be nicknamed "The Beehive State."

On the sunny afternoon of May 13, 1854, Jimmy blew out the candles on his birthday cake and made a wish. He was twelve now, and more than ever he wanted a horse.

While his mother sliced through the chocolate icing and layers of fluffy white cake, Jimmy stood next to her, savoring his wish. The yard was noisy with the laughter of his sisters, who chased each other and twirled in their long skirts.

Nine sisters, Jimmy sighed. He yearned for a brother with whom he could wrestle and climb trees or explore the outskirts of town. A brother would understand Jimmy's desire for adventure. A brother would understand why Jimmy hoped his birthday present would be a horse.

But the small, square package his father proudly handed him had nothing to do with a horse. Tucked inside the paper was a silver pocket watch, engraved with Jimmy's initials.

Mr. Spoon watched expectantly as Jimmy unfolded a note lined with elegant blue script. It was an announcement. Silently, Jimmy read the words.

He was now the honored Junior Partner at Spoon's

Fancy Store, where he would be in charge of polishing and arranging the pocket watches displayed under glass. Instead of smiling, as his father surely hoped he would, Jimmy closed his eyes and tried to hide his disappointment.

It was a job that he knew would be painfully quiet.

Already Jimmy's heart ached with boredom.

2

Indians

The morning air was cool. Jimmy stood in the yard
behind his house, listening to his older sisters in
the kitchen clearing breakfast from the table. Mother
was busy with the youngest girls and Father had
started his walk to the store, eight streets away down
Main Street.

Jimmy loved this hour. The sun was still behind
the dark Wasatch Mountains and he could hear
roosters crowing through the valley. He had finished
raking the stable, brushing the mare, and filling the
troughs with fresh water and hay. There was time
to run to his favorite spot. Time to enjoy being
outdoors before reporting to his father at half past
eight.

Beyond town, a boulder with a cavelike shelter
was nestled near an irrigation canal. Jimmy came
here often to think and to play war with stacks of
pebbles he'd flick at ants. He'd formed the Jimmy

Spoon Club with the boulder as secret headquarters, but so far he was the only member. There were plenty of boys around town, but most were occupied with school this early in the morning. Because Jimmy worked in his father's store, his lessons were postponed until after supper.

Jimmy listened. Had he heard someone approaching? A figure darted into the gully, and for a moment Jimmy felt a happy anticipation. Perhaps it was Robert Dean sneaking up for fun. Jimmy crouched, then inched his way around the boulder, keeping his head low and trying not to giggle. *At last a friend*, he thought, smiling.

But when he peeked over the side and saw who had made the noise, Jimmy froze. He was too startled to speak.

Two Shoshoni boys, older than Jimmy, stood a stride away. They were naked except for leather flaps around their waists and moccasins on their feet. Hair black as crow wings flowed over their shoulders. Each had a feather tied to the side of his head.

They stared at Jimmy. Jimmy stared back. Finally, one of the Indians raised his hand in greeting. "How d'ya do, white boy?"

Jimmy stood still. Indians, real Indians. He'd heard stories about scalpings and such, but for some

reason he didn't feel afraid. Secretly he was de-
lighted. He removed his hat.

"Reckon I better introduce myself. Jimmy Spoon,"
he said, pointing to his chest. "Jimmy." He was
proud of his good manners.

For several moments he watched their faces and
realized that even though they seemed stern, there
was no animosity. Maybe they would like to be in
his club.

Through gestures and a few words of English,
Jimmy learned their names were Nampa, which meant
moccasin, and Ga-mu, meaning rabbit. Nampa faced
north and whistled. A brown pony with patches of
white on its sides appeared from the distance. Another whistle and it trotted toward them.

Jimmy drew a deep breath. The pinto was the
most wonderful animal he'd ever seen. An eagle's
feather was tied to her forelock and a small beaded
pouch hung from her halter. He reached tentatively
to pet her jaw, then behind her fuzzy ear. A big
brown eye watched him.

"Easy, girl, easy," he said. Jimmy hugged the
pony's neck and breathed in her warm smell.
"Woooee, she's a beaut. I wish my pa would let me
have a horse like this." He looked at the boys' faces,
hoping they understood him.

Nampa responded by rocking his arms side to

side as if cradling an infant. Then he pantomimed wearing a dress.

"There's a baby?" Jimmy asked, bewildered.

Ga-mu pointed to Jimmy, then to the pinto. He pointed north, then touched the feather in his hair.

There were more gestures and broken English. Jimmy was at first confused, then he realized the boys were describing a mother. The mother of their chief. The boys wanted Jimmy to ride with them to their village to meet this mother of their chief.

Jimmy felt a small thrill. To ride a horse with real Indians would be an adventure, a wonderful adventure.

While he considered this extraordinary offer, the sun's first rays burst over the top of the mountain range. Jimmy's father would be tapping his foot with impatience by now.

"I gotta go, boys! I'll be back," he called over his shoulder.

For the first time in days, his heart lifted at the thought of tomorrow.

3

Full Moon

Three weeks passed. Every morning Jimmy met the Shoshoni boys beyond town. He pretended they were members of the Jimmy Spoon Club, even though he didn't know how to explain this to them.

Nampa and Ga-mu helped him mount the pretty horse, which he named Pinto Bean. Riding exhilarated him. Galloping with the wind and sun in his face made him feel free for the first time in his life. He liked the way the Indian boys let him take over, trusting him with the horse.

Jimmy was unable to forget that they wanted him to visit their tribe, especially after Nampa formed another word picture with his hands: if Jimmy rode to the village to meet their chief's mother, the horse would be his.

Jimmy pointed to Pinto Bean, then pressed his hand to his heart, imitating Nampa. The horse would be his?

Yes, Nampa nodded. The horse would be his.

Jimmy felt a wild excitement. Maybe if he asked his parents, they would let him go. He could meet the chief's mother, then return home. And he could keep the horse! It seemed simple enough—although Jimmy was puzzled as to why she wanted to meet *him*.

He also wasn't sure how far away the boys' village was. From their hand language, it seemed that it was about a two-hour ride.

What Jimmy *did* know was how badly he wanted to keep Pinto Bean and how he wanted to play with these boys all the time. He admired the ease with which they swung onto their horses and that they weren't buttoned into hot clothing. He wanted to be like them, to run outdoors all day long. Jimmy was sure they could hunt and fish any time they wanted.

Wide awake, Jimmy listened to the snoring of his father and the gentle breathing of his sisters and mother. Moonlight streamed through the window above the cupboard, illuminating the room.

Lucy slept in a cradle by his mother's side of the four-poster. Burrowed into the bed next to the spinning wheel were his four younger sisters: Rose, who was two; Annie, three; Frances, four; and Emma, five. Clara and Molly were old enough to be wives, fifteen and sixteen, but they seemed content living as daughters. They shared the trundle next to the fireplace with Nan, Jimmy's twin.

During the day their home bustled with activity and happy noises from the children, but an unspoken grief lingered, like a cobweb in an overhead rafter. Olivia, the eldest sister, had married Thomas Messersmith last year and moved into a cottage across the street. But on a bright, spring morning several months ago, Olivia bled to death after giving birth. Jimmy's mother wept, but afterwards there was only silence. The tragedy was never discussed.

Jimmy sat up on his cot. He liked his family. Sisters could be bossy, especially Clara, but overall they weren't too mean. But now that he'd tasted freedom with the Indian boys, his restlessness grew. How he wished his father were a rancher instead of a shopkeeper.

He lay awake until the moon passed and his mother rose to kindle the stove for breakfast. Candlelight revealed her leaning over the long, rough table with a rolling pin, flattening the dough that had risen overnight. Jimmy tiptoed across the plank floor and threw his arms around her waist.

"Oh, Mother," he cried into her apron. He didn't know how to tell her the burdens of his heart or that he was sorry about Olivia. She set the rolling pin down and held him. Jimmy didn't move until he heard his father unlatch the door and walk across the porch to the outhouse.

"Mother," he repeated, looking up to her face. Her auburn hair fell to her waist and he thought she had never seemed more beautiful. Many mornings he would rush to help her cut biscuits before his sisters awoke. He savored those early moments with her and, though it bothered him that she worked so hard, he wasn't sure how to help her more. Instead, he asked her about a horse.

"Do you think Pa will let me have one if I ask him again? I'll triple my chores and take charge of the garden and milking and fence-fixing if only he'd let me have my very own horse. All the other boys have horses . . ." Jimmy's words tumbled fast.

". . . and if only I didn't have to be in the store all day." He knew she was afraid of Indians so he didn't tell her about Nampa and Ga-mu. He couldn't ask her about visiting their village.

His mother sat on the bench and pulled him to her side. The candle on the table cast long shadows through the darkened room and made her face glow. When she whispered, the flame danced.

"You're his only son, Jimmy. He wants you to be like him, to take over the store when he gets old." She stroked the hair from his forehead. "He needs you. We all need you."

Lucy fussed in her cradle just as his father came in from the yard, stretching suspenders over his shoulders. When he saw Jimmy sitting, he frowned.

"Chores," was all he said.

Three women in long summer dresses admired the parasols hanging from a rafter. A man with mutton-chop sideburns rocked on his heels, examining a pipe. Jimmy's father smiled pleasantly at his customers. His hair was parted on his forehead and slicked to the sides with olive oil, a luxury item he sold for a dollar-fifty per bottle.

Red, white, and blue streamers were draped along the walls, and American flags with the thirty-one stars were clustered in the windows to celebrate next week's Fourth of July parade. Soon everything would be festive and noisy, but right now it was quiet, too quiet. The steady tick-ticking of watches under the glass case rose above the ladies' murmurings and, to Jimmy, it was a dreadful sound: minutes were passing.

"Father," he blurted. All heads turned toward Jimmy. He looked down at his boots. "Could I talk to you, please?" he said softly.

In the back room, surrounded by ceiling-high shelves, Jimmy sighed the deepest sigh of his life. Mr. Spoon's thumbs were hooked in his vest pockets, his fingers drumming impatiently against the brown satin. He looked at Jimmy's chin as he spoke.

"If I've said it once, I've said it a hundred times, you will have a horse when you turn fourteen years of age, not a day sooner. You are far too immature to have full responsibility for anything that requires so much attention."

"But Father," Jimmy whispered, "I'm twelve. Surely twelve is old enough . . ."

"Fourteen." Mr. Spoon turned to leave the room. "Not a day sooner." Jimmy hadn't had a chance to ask about meeting the chief's mother.

Three nights later, when the moon was full, Jimmy slipped away from his sleeping family. *I'll just be gone a day, long enough for them to miss me*, he thought. *Long enough to earn the pinto.* He was taking a chance that his father would let him keep it.

Nampa and Ga-mu were waiting at the edge of town with their horses. Pinto Bean was adorned with a red blanket under an elk-horn saddle that had no stirrups. There were feathers in her mane.

Fastened near the cantle was a *parfleche*, a square of deerhide folded like an envelope. It was beaded and full of dried berries and meat.

"Eee-up!" the Shoshoni boys shouted and they were off, galloping across a dry riverbed, north, into the moonlit night.

4

Saddle Sore

The boys rode fast, slowing only a few times to rest the horses. When they reached the north end of the Great Salt Lake, a blush of rose was spreading in the sky over the eastern mountains. Nampa signaled they would stop to eat.

But when Jimmy tried to dismount, he was so stiff and sore, he crumbled to the desert floor.

"My legs hurt. They're bleeding," he cried.

Jimmy tried to take his pants off, but they were stuck to his legs with dried blood. The Indian boys slit the cotton with their knives then peeled it carefully away. From his calves up to his bottom, Jimmy's skin was as raw as fresh meat.

Nampa and Ga-mu motioned that Jimmy should soak in the lake. His wounds would heal quickly from this water.

Too distressed to argue, Jimmy leaned until he fell in. He came up sputtering, eyes wide.

"Lordy!" he screamed. "Blazes! I'm dying right now, O Lordy!" He bucked and rolled on the shore, crying in pain. The salt stung and kept on stinging.

Worn out and miserable, Jimmy began to weep. He was embarrassed to cry in front of the boys, but he couldn't stop. How sorry he was he'd left Mother. And he was sorry too, for being so angry with Father. He cried for their worry, he cried about his hurt legs, and he cried thinking he might miss the Fourth of July parade. Several hours had passed since he'd sneaked away, yet the Indian village was nowhere in sight.

Ga-mu spread a buffalo robe in some tall grass, eased Jimmy onto it, then put another blanket over him. Jimmy cried himself to sleep.

He woke to the sun on his face and the smell of cooking. The Indians sat in front of a small fire. Jimmy watched as Nampa lifted a duck, coated with dried mud, from the coals with tongs made from bare twigs. When it had cooled, Nampa cracked the mud shell with a rock. The duck's skin and feathers dropped off in chunks, leaving the steaming, clean meat.

Come eat, they gestured when they noticed he was awake. It was still early morning.

Jimmy stood, but he whimpered from the soreness. They coaxed him. His knees wouldn't bend, so he walked stiltlike to the fire and, still standing, ate some duck. Hot juice dripped off his chin. He felt better.

The horses were ready. Nampa laid his buffalo robe in Pinto Bean's saddle then lifted Jimmy onto it. Jimmy was wearing only his shirt, as his hat had disappeared somewhere during the midnight run, and he'd lost his boots near the lake. Ga-mu folded a blanket over Jimmy's lap to keep the sun from burning his bare legs. The blanket also eased Jimmy's embarrassment, for he felt dreadfully exposed without any pants.

All day they traveled over country that looked like the bottom of a dried lake. Heat shimmered off the desert floor. Jimmy was so thirsty his head hurt and his lips were swollen. Nampa stopped to pick up some pebbles then showed Jimmy how to put one under his tongue. Jimmy's mouth soon watered. It was like having a small drink. He spat the pebble out.

Finally, at sunset the air began to cool and they found a spring. A full day had passed. Jimmy was worried. He had thought the boys said the ride would take just two hours, but they still hadn't reached the village. Jimmy was too tired and in too much pain to think clearly, to consider turning back on his own.

Nampa, who was taller and stronger than Gamu, lifted Jimmy from his horse, tucked him into a robe, and carried him to a boulder where he could rest. A fire inside a ring of rocks warmed him as the Shoshoni boys speared fish from the bank. Trout broiled over the coals made the finest supper Jimmy had eaten in a long time.

His eyes grew heavy. Before he drifted off to sleep, he noticed the canopy of stars. A breeze felt cool on his face, but the fur around him was soft and warm.

At dawn the three boys finished the fish and the dried elk meat that Nampa carried in the small pouch that hung from his waist. Then they rode until the sun was overhead. In the distance there flowed a broad, shallow river where dozens of horses were drinking. A few tipis stood on the bank beyond.

Jimmy had never seen an Indian village before. Suddenly he felt nervous. Soon he would meet a chief and the chief's mother. What if they didn't like him? he worried. What if they wouldn't let him keep the pinto after all?

As he squinted in the bright sunlight, hoping to

see some sign of friendliness, Nampa and Ga-mu whooped their horses into a gallop. Jimmy's legs rubbed miserably as he bounced along.

When they neared the camp, packs of barking dogs came out to escort them. Children surrounded the boys and stared at Jimmy Spoon. He felt uneasy around so many Indians, and he was humiliated to be without his trousers.

The boys led Jimmy on horseback through the camp to a tall tipi. In front of the opening stood a large Indian wearing fringed leggings and a cloth vest. He held a twelve-foot lance. Eagle feathers dangled from its tip like a banner.

Chief Washakie nodded his approval.

5

A New Family

An old woman held her arms out to Jimmy. She was round and short with a striped blanket over her shoulders. She seemed to want to hold him, but he couldn't move from the saddle.

Nampa spoke rapidly to her, and Jimmy could tell he was explaining about his skinned legs.

Washakie plunged his lance into the ground. He lifted Jimmy from the horse and carried him into the tipi. Walking to the left, he circled the fire until he came to the north side, where he laid him on a robe. Jimmy was unaware of the honor this meant. The robe was the chief's own bed.

The woman stepped in through the open flap and asked Jimmy a question. He looked at her blankly. She smiled, then bent over the cooking pouch that hung from a low tripod that straddled the fire. With a shaped buffalo horn, she ladled soup into a wooden bowl then held it to Jimmy's lips.

He drank. Chunks of tender deer meat melted in his mouth. How good it tasted! *Such a nice old woman*, Jimmy thought, *kind, like Mother.*

After he had eaten, Old Mother put her hand over Jimmy's heart and spoke to him tenderly, her words foreign but somehow comforting.

She rubbed his sores with skunk oil and mint. Even though her touch was gentle, Jimmy winced in pain. She covered him with a soft fur, then left him to rest.

Alone in the huge cone-shaped tent, Jimmy counted twenty-one tall poles pointing upward to where they crisscrossed, forming a smoke hole. Blue sky showed through above.

Jimmy looked around. Twenty hides were patched together and stretched over the poles, the hem stopping a few inches above the ground. On his side of the tipi, household sacks and sleeping robes weighted down a leather lining that reached a third of the way up the side.

The space between the cover and lining was as wide as the lodge poles and acted as a chimney flue. Warm air rising through the opening bore away smoke from the cooking fire.

Jimmy watched an edge of a white cloud drift past the blue above. He could hear water from the stream, a dog barking in the distance, and the sounds of children.

That afternoon, a girl of about fifteen—Clara's age—came into the lodge and sat next to Old Mother. She held a papoose sleeping in a cradleboard, which she propped against a pole. Jimmy learned that her name was Hanabi and that she was the chief's wife.

He watched as Old Mother unrolled a hide and spread it out at her knees. Jimmy found himself staring. The fingertips on Old Mother's left hand were missing. He felt sick inside. *She must have had a horrible accident*, he thought.

Despite the swollen stumps, she worked deftly with her knife, cutting the hide, then threading a bone needle with sinew. Hanabi, too, was sewing. When Old Mother held up a long shirt, he knew he was to get dressed. He felt greatly relieved—he hated being naked from his waist down.

The shirt hung loose, with soft fringe at his knees and sleeves. Hanabi tied a strip of leather around his waist, then opened a pair of moccasins for him to step into. He had never felt clothes so soft and warm before, but he wondered about pants. It was breezy without them.

Jimmy didn't completely understand Old Mother's explanation, but he figured she wanted his legs to heal before he wore pants.

Old Mother led him outside. The afternoon sun was bright. Soon the children were crowding around him, staring. He looked at their faces. Everyone had brown eyes and dark hair; some wore their hair over their shoulders, some wore braids with greased pompadours. They were dressed in a variety of leather shirts, open vests, and long breechcloths.

Jimmy tried a smile. The girls giggled behind their hands. A boy named Poog stepped forward with a stick. He had heard about Jimmy's raw legs and he wanted to see for himself.

Before Jimmy realized what was happening, Poog had lifted his new shirt with the stick, high enough to show everyone Jimmy's naked parts.

Laughter burst from the children. Jimmy was frightened. Without thinking, he kicked Poog in the leg as hard as he could; the kick landed Poog cheek-down in the dirt.

Suddenly a large, screaming woman pushed her way into the ring of children. It was Poog's mother.

She stuck her face right up to Jimmy's, their noses almost touching. He felt the sharp tip of her knife against his throat. His knees went weak with fear. He wanted to cry.

His mother had never raised her voice to him, yet here was a mother ready to kill him.

"*Iki, iki,*" said Old Mother, running to his side. *Right here*, she was saying to the angry woman. *He is my little son.* Calmly she walked Jimmy back to

the tipi, where she gave him a patty of dried serviceberries. It tasted like a cookie.

The next day another boy tried to raise the dress.
When Jimmy kicked him, the boy let out a scream
that brought half the camp rushing for a look.

Chief Washakie stood quietly by his lodge. When
they noticed him watching, there was silence.

After that day, the children left Jimmy's dress
alone.

6

Travel

When Jimmy had been with the Shoshoni for three days, he realized his family would think he'd run away. He felt anguish knowing that his mother was worrying, and he was mad that he would miss the Fourth of July parade.

These feelings confused him. Perhaps riding off with Nampa and Ga-mu had been too much mischief for a boy his age. He had thought he could return home any time he wanted, but an unpleasant reality sent a chill through him:

Jimmy was deep in Indian country. He did not know how to find his way home.

After two weeks, Jimmy's legs had healed enough for him to ride horseback. Washakie called for the tipis to be taken down at the next sunrise and the horses to be packed for travel.

When the herd was brought in from grazing and

Jimmy saw Pinto Bean, he hugged her neck as if he'd found a lost friend. She made it easier not to think about his family for now.

He liked sitting high on his own horse. His leggings were soft and kept him from being sunburned. His new shirt was loose enough to let air in through the sleeves and neck. A fur robe was rolled behind his saddle and a new pouch dangled from either side: one filled with dried berries, the other with strips of smoked buffalo meat. Old Mother didn't want Jimmy to feel hunger. Like the others, he carried a personal horn spoon in his belongings.

They traveled fifteen miles, an easy ride for Jimmy, then camped along a stream they called *Koheets*. Jimmy was beginning to understand bits of their language, so when Old Mother told him to wash himself, he hesitated, remembering the pain of the salt bath.

She dipped a tin cup into the water and drank to show it was fresh.

He untied his moccasins and tossed his pants on the sandy beach. He left his long shirt on. When he waded out he laughed, then dunked himself. The water was cool; it felt wonderful. His shirt clung to his skin. Later it would dry, feeling tight at first, then stretching for a perfect fit.

Washakie watched from shore, smiling.

Over the next three days the band traveled north, stopping in the late afternoons so the women could erect the stick tents and start the cooking fires with dried buffalo droppings. By dawn each day, the tipi covers would flutter to the ground, the *travois* and horses would be packed, and the slow migration would begin again. Jimmy noticed that many rode bareback.

On the fourth day they passed Fort Hall and came to a large, fast river called *Piupa*, a river white men had named the Snake in 1812. Several other Shoshoni were camped there, ready for a friendly reunion.

The women tied bundles of bulrushes together to build rafts wide enough to float robes, cooking gear, sacks of jerky, and small children across the river. The men and boys swam their horses to the other side, drifting into a flat beach.

Jimmy begged to ride Pinto Bean across, but Old Mother refused.

During the seven days it took to get everyone safely across the *Piupa*, Jimmy had more fun than he'd ever had in his life.

He ate whenever he was hungry and got as wet as he wanted without being told he'd catch his death of a cold. Old Mother gave him a fish-hook and a line made from a strand of Pinto Bean's tail. Jimmy caught his first fish, a large speckled trout as big as his arm.

Other boys became friendly and they played together. Jimmy ran and whooped as loud as he wanted. He was enjoying himself too much to remember Spoon's Fancy Store or that his parents might be frantic.

Old Mother kept close watch on him, worried that Jimmy might kick someone. She wanted no more camp fights over her new son.

The more Jimmy played with the children, the more he understood what they were saying to him. Although Shoshoni sounded strange on his tongue, he was soon repeating short phrases. He felt like a real Indian. If only he could wear a feather in his hair.

7

New Hunting Grounds

Late August brought hot days and frosty nights. The tipis glowed like lanterns under the black sky.

Washakie's band now camped in the Big Hole Basin. In the east a range of mountains rose white with snow. Years earlier, French fur trappers had named these peaks *Les Trois Tetons*, "the three breasts." The Shoshoni called them *Teewinot*, meaning many pinnacles.

Jimmy guessed a prairie fire had swept through the basin, because the grassland and foothills were black. But as the band moved farther into the valley, he saw there was movement within the black, like the slow roll of gravy in a pan.

The Indians were now pointing, excited. Old Mother leaned down from her horse and patted the bundle behind Jimmy's saddle.

Bojono. Buffalo.

As far as Jimmy could see, there were *bojono*

grazing; brown, shaggy beasts unworried by the approaching strangers. The last time Jimmy had seen a buffalo was on the plains east of Utah Territory. His father's wagon train had stopped for five days to shoot as many as possible in order to make winter coats from the fur. But that herd had looked like a patch on the prairie compared to this blanket spreading into the distance.

As the women raised the tipis, the men readied themselves for the hunt. Spears and arrows were checked for straightness, and the fastest horses were led to the stream to drink, then rest.

At first light the next morning, two dozen hunters rode off. Jimmy had seen flintlock rifles wrapped with rawhide and brass tacks, many of them protected by beaded scabbards, along with the spears. He wondered when he and Pinto Bean would be able to join in the action. Nothing could be finer than loping alongside a *bojono*, back straight and feather in his hair, effortlessly shooting arrows into the animal's side.

By afternoon the hunters had returned and their wives, mothers, and sisters rode out to skin the animals. Even though the boys Jimmy's age stayed in camp, Old Mother insisted Jimmy ride with her. He trotted along on Pinto Bean, wishing he had his own spear in case a big one wandered by.

The women recognized their husbands' arrows and each one knew which *bojono* to work on. They laughed if their men had used too many arrows, planning to tease them later about being papooses, not mighty hunters.

When Jimmy stood next to a fallen bull, he was surprised at its size. It lay in the sagebrush, its massive head as high as Jimmy's waist, its furry side round and taller than Jimmy's cheek. He could hide behind it and still be standing.

Old Mother and Hanabi first sliced the belly open, then steadily cut the hide away. They peeled the fur off six animals and laid the skins in the sun bloody side up while they sectioned the meat. By roping a buffalo's hind hooves to their ponies' saddles, the women could roll the animal over to work on its other side.

By sundown, dozens of *travois* were loaded high for the return to camp. Nothing was left on the plain but splotches of blood and clumps of flattened sagebrush. Each horn, hoof, and tassled tail was taken, along with the hides and meat. The girls carried baskets filled with *bojono* chips, the dropping that produced hot, smokeless fires perfect for inside the tipis.

For several days the hunters relaxed in the warm August sun while the women and girls sliced meat into thin strips to hang over racks outside. Flies stayed away from the meat because the strips were too thin for them to implant their eggs. When the strips were almost dry, the women pounded them between two rocks until they became soft, then hung them to stiffen once more.

"*Ta-oh,*" Old Mother said as she handed Jimmy a piece. The jerky was dusty and tough to chew, but it tasted good.

The camp was fragrant with the aroma of meat roasting, stews bubbling, and wood smoke from the many outdoor fires. As Jimmy wandered among the tipis, he could also smell rotting food that had been tossed aside for the dogs. And in the bushes beyond camp, a bad odor reminded him of an outhouse.

Jimmy played along the stream with the other boys, throwing rocks at fish and skipping flat pebbles across the water. The women and girls staked the *bojono* hides fur side down to scrape them clean.

By early September they had traveled north to Deer Lodge Valley in what white men would soon call Montana Territory. Now there were close to three thousand Shoshoni gathered, including the *Too-koo-ree-keys,* or Sheepeaters. Jimmy was thrilled by the sight of so many tipis lining the stream as far as he could see, all their doorways opening to the east.

Dogs, horses, and boisterous children covered the countryside. Jimmy saw no other white person, not even a fur trader.

Old Mother tailed Jimmy as he explored, worried that he'd get lost. He could now understand most of their language, even though he still found it easier to respond in English.

When Old Mother told Jimmy that White Plume's band liked to steal white boys and eat them, he knew she meant Chief Pocatello. Jimmy suspected she was teasing but, still, he didn't leave Old Mother's side.

The thundering of hooves drew his attention to a grassy flat where braves were racing bareback, their hair streaming behind them, piercing the air with their whoops. Jimmy guessed they were probably betting on the races after he saw one brave rounding up fifty ponies he'd apparently won.

Old Mother pulled Jimmy away from the crowd as the racing grew louder and wilder. By sundown two Indians had been trampled to death, and a bucking horse had kicked a woman with her cradleboard, killing the baby.

For several days the cries of mourners pierced the air.

Jimmy was uneasy with this loud display of grief. He stayed close to Old Mother, glad she was there to protect him.

8

The Scalp Dance

Bonfires dotted the valley under a moonless sky. Drums pounded. A high-pitched singing rose in the night air, making Jimmy shiver; the voices sounded like a wail.

In the center of camp, warriors circled the largest fire, the bells on their moccasins jingling loudly between drumbeats. Their faces, arms, and chests were painted and feathers decorated their hair. To Jimmy's horror, some held spears in the air, dangling scalps from a recent raid on a wagon train.

Jimmy clamped his hand over his mouth and swallowed the bile rising in his throat. He had heard about such things, but he hadn't thought friendly Indians killed people. A sickening, sweet odor brought tears to his eyes. He was afraid and angry at the same time.

Just that afternoon, Jimmy had played happily at the river with the other children. When Ga-mu introduced him to a quiet girl named Nahanee, Jimmy had blushed. Nahanee was pretty. Her deerskin dress fell softly to her knees; her feet were bare and brown. She had smiled shyly at him, then looked down. Jimmy had been too tongue-tied with joy to even say hello. But now *this*—this atrocity—on the same day! Jimmy felt ashamed for having had so much fun among people who could be so savage.

He counted six scalps, all caked with blood. One was a woman's long red hair, one a girl's blond pigtails, four were men's scalps, three dark, one gray.

Jimmy thought about his family. His little sisters wore pigtails, his Uncle Lefty had gray hair. Molly's hair was long and flowing. He pictured their house pierced with burning arrows and his mother crying for help. Why had he left them? They needed him and he wasn't there. He hated himself for thinking that living with Indians would be carefree.

If only he were home! He would be good to the toddlers and he wouldn't sass Clara ever again. Jimmy wanted to escape.

Washakie's Indians danced with scalps from the Crow tribe. Only Pocatello's men had killed white settlers. The warriors stuck a tall pole in the ground and strung the scalps to it. They danced and shrieked. It was the most horrible noise Jimmy had ever heard.

Leaders of the different bands circled, lifting one knee high, then the other, bending at the waist over and over. In a larger ring around them, the warriors danced. Soon the women put on their husbands' warbonnets and started their own dance in a larger circle outside the men's.

Jimmy ran to his tipi.

The dancing continued all night and the next day and the next.

9

Kidnapped

Summer was over. The air turned cooler, the days shorter. The snows were not far off. Fewer tipis stood along the stream as the bands of Shoshoni began breaking camp, the various chiefs leading their families to winter sites.

Jimmy was relieved to be among just a few households again, safe from so many strangers staring at his white skin. It was getting easier not to think about his parents and sisters—although, when he did, he felt a small ache inside.

In spite of his disgust for the scalp dance, each passing day found Jimmy more at home with the Indians. The idea of running away had faded. He feared being alone in the wilderness and he was beginning to fear his father's anger if he did return.

Jimmy felt paralyzed by confusion. It was simply easier for him to do nothing. *When I'm ready*, he resolved, *I'll ask Nampa and Ga-mu to take me home.*

After Pocatello's group had left, Washakie called for the women to pack while he and the others rounded up the horses.

Jimmy looked all over for Pinto Bean, but she was nowhere to be found. Jimmy was heartbroken. Forgetting Old Mother's warnings, he sneaked away while she was gathering firewood.

Just outside camp Jimmy met some hunters. They hadn't seen Pinto Bean.

He hurried along a trail that led into a pine forest. A tall Indian had just snared a rabbit and was mounting his horse. Yes, he had seen the spotted one, just through the woods over the ridge with some other hunters. He pulled Jimmy into the saddle behind him.

"We will find your pony."

But when they rode beyond the trees to a clearing, there was no horse in sight and no other hunters. Suddenly the rider kicked into a gallop, his legs flying out from the horse's sides. Jimmy was terrified.

He clung to the man's waist and tried to squeeze his legs tight so he wouldn't fall.

"Stop, please!" he cried. "Where are you going?"

As they rode farther from camp, Jimmy's heart pounded with fear. Why hadn't he listened to Old

Mother? *They're going to kill me and dance around my scalp*, he thought, filled with panic.

"Stop!"

But the Indian only whipped his horse harder. The horse's hooves kicked up chunks of mud as it sped on.

Jimmy didn't want to be captured by White Plume. He tried to think. The only way to escape was to jump, but the horse was moving too fast. It was also much taller than Pinto Bean; it would be a long fall to the ground.

But jumping was his only chance. He waited. A grove of aspen was up ahead. It came closer.

The horse began to slow down among the trees.

Jimmy reached up with both hands.

Now!

He grabbed a low branch. The instant he did, his body jerked out of the saddle. He crashed onto the trail and scrambled as fast as he could toward camp, glancing over his shoulder.

The Indian had already reined his horse around and was in a fierce gallop, lasso twirling in the air.

The rope landed over Jimmy's neck and under one arm, dragging him several yards. The man hit him with his quirt. Jimmy lay in the dirt, stunned.

"Get on or I will put an arrow through you!"

"Please," Jimmy begged, but again he was

whipped across the shoulders. Finally Jimmy stood and let the Indian pull him onto the horse.

They rode hard. Jimmy wanted to bite the man on his back or kick him. He had to get away. This might be his last chance and he didn't care if he died trying.

With adrenaline pumping furiously through him, Jimmy grabbed one of the warrior's braids, gave it a mighty jerk, and leapt off the horse. When they hit the ground Jimmy ran for the brush. He turned to see the Indian hook an arrow onto his bow and aim. Suddenly—and unexpectedly—the man whirled, took a running jump onto the horse, and raced in the opposite direction.

Several Shoshoni were riding fast toward Jimmy, Washakie in the lead. Without stopping, Washakie leaned low to grab Jimmy around the waist and swoop him in front of the saddle. They sped toward home.

Old Mother waited on the trail outside camp. When she saw Jimmy was safe, she wept. Then she scolded him.

"I thought I would never see my little son again," she said. "White Plume's warriors wanted a white boy to sell for many ponies."

"But my horse . . ."

"The hunters found your horse," Washakie said. He was twice as tall as Jimmy. His salt-and-pepper hair hung loose over his shoulders. A single feather lay at the back of his head today, signifying he was a leader.

"The hunters showed me where you had gone. Don't ever chase after your horse alone, *Dawii*, Young Brother. There are many things in the woods waiting for a boy who thinks he knows much."

Sixty tipis were taken down the next morning and packed. Washakie's band had four hundred horses and dozens of dogs, most of them half-breed coyotes. Jimmy had noticed the dogs were not usually considered pets and they were not used for food; they were just noisy tagalongs, always sniffing for food.

The Shoshoni fanned out in different directions for the winter. It would be easier for smaller groups to find game and firewood.

As Jimmy lashed together Old Mother's lodge poles, a girl watched him from behind a *travois*. She blushed when he noticed her.

"Hello, Nahanee." His face felt warm when he said her name, and he felt a happy ache inside. She was even prettier than the first time he'd seen her.

1 0

Learning to Hunt

Travel was slow. Jimmy rode alongside Old Mother, sometimes dropping back to be near Hanabi. He liked to look at Oddo, the papoose on her back, who was as snug as a baby could be. Her wide brown eyes smiled when Jimmy made faces at her, reminding him of baby Lucy.

That night they camped at the base of a canyon. As Jimmy watched the firelight inside the tipi, Old Mother revealed there was a surprise for him.

Washakie reached behind his backrest. A small bow made of chokecherry wood came out first, then a narrow quiver made from stiff deerhide, adorned with colored porcupine quills. Six long arrows with feathered ends were inside. Washakie walked around the circle clockwise to where Jimmy sat, careful not to pass between the fire and the others.

Jimmy couldn't believe it. His very own bow and arrows.

For an instant he wanted to throw his arms around Washakie's neck and cling to him with gratitude. Instead, he cast his eyes down to show respect. "Thank you," Jimmy said softly.

Now he was like a real Indian. This was the best thing that could have happened to the Jimmy Spoon Club. To have a real bow and real arrows meant that his club was in good form. Maybe Jimmy would shoot a big bear, and then he could make a claw necklace for Nahanee.

Before sunrise, Washakie took Jimmy to watch the hunters run antelope. About fifty men on horseback circled the animals and took turns chasing them. Nampa and Ga-mu herded runaways.

Finally the antelope were so exhausted they hid their heads under a bush and lay in the dirt, resigned to their fate. Even though Jimmy felt sorry for the animals, he shot at them with his bow. Washakie showed him how to hook the arrow onto the sinew string, then pull his elbow straight back.

This was hard for Jimmy and took many tries. Finally, he killed an antelope.

"Oh boy! Did you see me?" Jimmy couldn't contain his excitement.

In camp, Old Mother prepared a feast.

"My little son is a hunter," she bragged to everyone.

After several days of travel, Washakie's band camped where they could see *bojono* and butterscotch-colored antelope grazing for miles in every direction.

"You may now go, as often as you like, with Washakie while he hunts. Learn his ways," Old Mother said to Jimmy. Never before had he felt so lucky, especially when Washakie spoke to the hunters that night around the fire.

"Dawii, my young brother, is a big hunter now, but his bow is for a child."

An elder leaned forward into the warm light. His name was Mozo, which meant whisker. He wore a feather by his ear and a necklace of elk teeth. His braids were silvery gray.

"I am old and my eyes are dim," Mozo said. "Your *dawii* may have my best bow."

It was a fine, strong bow, standing up to Jimmy's chin. Another elder gave him eight arrows made from cherrywood. Jimmy was so proud, he wanted to make a speech.

"Next time, I'll kill a whole herd of *bojono*," he boasted.

"I know you will, Dawii," said Old Mother. Her

blanket covered her shoulders, opening to calm hands in her lap. "But tell me, what will you do with all that meat?"

Washakie nodded. He lifted a coal from the fire with a forked stick, then dropped it into the bowl of his pipe. It was a small pipe made from red stone. After a puff and several long moments he spoke.

"Dawii, you are just like the *tybo* who shoot all the *bojono* they see, then leave them on the prairie for wolves and crows."

Jimmy knew *tybo* meant white people, men like his father and other settlers. He felt a blush of shame.

"This is not our way. The Great Spirit would be unhappy with us. We would have bad luck and we would go hungry if we killed animals when we didn't need to."

Jimmy watched Hanabi gather kindling near a fallen oak. She had a blanket slung over her shoulders to hold baby Oddo, who was wrapped snugly inside with just the top of her fuzzy black hair showing.

This reminded him of his mother. It seemed she always had an infant in one arm and a toddler grabbing her skirt while she performed a chore. *Tybo* women might think they had nothing in common with Indian women, but Jimmy could see that wasn't so.

All mothers are busy, he decided. *They are busy and they look tired.* It also seemed to him that Shoshoni men and boys had all the fun. He felt he should bring this to the chief's attention.

". . . and most of the women carry a papoose on their backs all day," he complained. "I'm glad I'm not a girl! Don't you fellas ever carry firewood?"

Washakie listened. The fall air was cool. He sat cross-legged against the sunny side of his lodge, a smile on his face. He was amused by his young brother.

"Women work hard. Men work hard. If our dear Old Mother could bring down ten *bojono* in one sun, I would carry water for her and sew moccasins.

"If mothers ride off to hunt or fight enemies, who will nurse their babies? Who will sing cradle songs?"

Jimmy was embarrassed. He had observed his new family, but he hadn't tried to understand them.

"Well, how come you get to walk in front all the time, and Hanabi follows? My mother would burn my pa's ears if she always went second." Jimmy was remembering how the men in his town like to tip their hats and say "Ladies first."

"A new trail has high grass where snakes hide, and there are thorns. It is safer for the man to go first. When the snows are deep, the first walker makes the path easier for the ones behind." Washakie closed his eyes and lifted his face to the sun, enjoying its warmth.

"Dawii," he finally said. "If I fill my arms with firewood, as you suggest, and strap a cradleboard over my shoulders, how will I pull an arrow on an enemy who hides in the trees?"

Jimmy didn't answer.

"A boy who is patient learns much," he said. "An owl listening from his branch has more wisdom than a magpie who chatters all day long."

11

Winter 1854

Snow fell in the mountains. Hanabi and her friends sewed Jimmy warm leggings and a shirt. New moccasins came up to his knees; the insides were soft with rabbit fur and the outer hide had come from the top of an old tipi cover, blackened and waterproofed from many cooking fires.

Old Mother made him a cape from one of the *bojono* Washakie had killed. It fastened in front with the smooth, round tip of an elk antler. A pattern of colored beads adorned the front of his shirt. Fringe dangled from the sleeves and ruffled when he ran.

"Like a feather in the wind," Old Mother observed.

Jimmy had never seen such fine clothes nor had he ever felt so warm. He liked the hat Old Mother made from muskrat skin. It peaked on top and had two rabbit tails sewn on each side for tassels.

The other children weren't dressed quite as

splendidly as Jimmy, but after all, he reasoned, he was *dawii* to Chief Washakie. He felt important when everyone called him "young brother."

They were camped near a partly frozen river below high buttes. Fifty years earlier, the white explorers Meriwether Lewis and William Clark had named it Jefferson River, but to Washakie it was *Paitapa.*

Hunters brought in twenty elk and three bears who had been sleeping in their dens. The cold had driven the *bojono* to their winter range near the steaming hot pools by Yellowstone River. Several strays wandered near camp. Their thick fur was crusted with snow, and icicles hung below their bellies, clinking like the delicate glass chimes Jimmy had heard in Brigham Young's courtyard.

Jimmy hurried into the tipi for his bow and arrows. When he crouched behind a log to aim, Washakie's hand fell on his shoulder.

"We are warm and we have *ta-oh* to last until the snows melt." He pointed to the forest, where two white-tailed deer nibbled at some bark.

"The Great Spirit will provide fresh meat when we need it."

Snow had fallen steadily all night and the drifts were waist deep as Jimmy searched for firewood. He was cold. His moccasins were tight below his knees yet dampness had managed to creep in.

His hands were numb and his runny nose had made ice above his lip. He felt cranky and tired from a head cold. Living with Indians was not always the fun he had thought it would be. He missed his mother's warm kitchen. He even missed working alongside his father in the quiet store.

When he returned to the lodge, his arms loaded with kindling, Old Mother greeted him with a smile. She was kneeling in her customary spot by the fire, a robe of fur over her shoulders.

She held out a small square of deerhide. On it were pieces of shredded meat with a sweet aroma. "Something new for you to try," she said proudly.

Jimmy took it from her and sniffed the meat. He handed it back to her.

"It is for you to eat," she said. Old Mother nodded for him to take a bite. As she watched him expectantly, he lifted the meat to his lips. The smell bothered him. He frowned.

"Don't worry, Dawii. It is only *yaha* cooked with roots."

Yaha! Jimmy didn't know Indians ate the yellow-bellied marmot, especially during winter when it hibernated. He started to hand it back to her, but the hopeful look in her eyes made him change his mind. He knew she would be insulted if he refused the food.

He took a bite. A small bite. He pictured a cat-sized marmot romping through the meadow then standing on its hind legs to whistle. Jimmy's tongue moved the greasy meat in his mouth, side to side, any place to avoid swallowing it, but suddenly, gulp, down it slid. It tasted like rich pork, a taste he didn't like at all. His throat tightened and, with a violent shiver, he vomited into his lap.

"Aaagh!" Repulsed by the mess and embarrassed, he began to cry. He wiped his mouth with his sleeve then tried to clean his legs.

"I've never tasted anything so . . ." How could Jimmy explain? He surprised himself by yelling at Old Mother, fast, and in English. She couldn't understand his words, but she understood his face.

He punched the tent flap open and launched himself into the snow. He tumbled against the buckskin legs of someone who'd been listening. Jimmy looked up.

"Washakie," he whispered.

It was starting to snow again. White flakes fell against the chief's braids and coated the dark fur of his robe. For several long moments he stared at Jimmy. Then he turned toward his lodge. Jimmy was afraid to move. He was shivering with cold.

When Washakie returned, a quiver of arrows was strapped across his chest and he cradled a bow made from white cedar. He walked to the edge of the woods, then waited for Jimmy.

Is he going to punish me? Jimmy wondered. Panic fluttered in his heart. Why hadn't he stayed with his own family? The worst would be a thrashing with his father's razor strap, and right now Jimmy would settle for ten of those. He felt afraid even though he'd always known Washakie to be kind.

Reluctantly, Jimmy followed Washakie to a grove of aspens. The white branches were bare, with dark ripples in the bark. In the distance the horses huffed and pawed for new grass. Poog stood in the corral, watching. Knowing he was being observed deepened Jimmy's humiliation.

The chief faced Jimmy. The two eagle feathers in his hair today signified his marriage to Hanabi, and Jimmy felt sad that he'd never live to see his own wedding day. *It will be lonely dying in the snow*, he thought.

"Dawii, your words have pierced our Old Mother."

"I'll tell her I am sorry. I will do it right now." Jimmy wanted more than anything to run back to their lodge and bury his face in Old Mother's warm arms. "She'll forgive me. I know she will."

Washakie hooked an arrow onto the string of his

bow and handed it to Jimmy. He nodded toward the nearest aspen.

"Shoot that tree."

Jimmy's fingers were stiff around the bow and he was shaking from cold and from terror. He aimed, pulled his arm back, and let go. The arrow drifted to the ground at his feet.

Washakie pulled another arrow from his quiver. The shaft was painted with red stripes and the short feathers on its end were black. Jimmy aimed again. The arrow thwanged as it hit the trunk and stuck.

"Take the arrow out," commanded Washakie. Jimmy was mystified. He walked slowly to the tree. He pulled hard, wiggling it a bit, then it popped free. *Now he's going to shoot me*, he thought.

Washakie stood beside Jimmy and took his hand. He pressed Jimmy's fingers against the hole in the tree.

"Now remove the hole, Dawii."

Jimmy closed his eyes. He understood.

1 2

Girl Trouble

Winter passed slowly.

"Mother Earth sleeps under her blanket of snow," Old Mother explained. She sang to baby Oddo, told stories to Jimmy, and showed him how to keep warm by coating his skin with bear grease. The extreme cold forced children to play in their lodges.

Finally a wind from the south brought a welcome change. Jimmy's lungs didn't hurt as much when he breathed in the frosty air. The snow *crunched* underfoot rather than *squeaked* as it had in the subzero temperatures. Spring was not far off.

Jimmy ran on snowshoes with Ga-mu. They stopped at the edge of a frozen river where Nampa waited beside a small fire.

Ga-mu lifted a rock the size of a porcupine and heaved it onto the ice. It crashed through to the river bottom, leaving a wide fishing hole.

Before long, others had crowded around with sticks, lines, and hooks. Jimmy was amazed to see trout swimming slowly below the ice as if it were a lazy summer day. An otter surfaced to take a breath, then dove. It scooted playfully among submerged rocks, then appeared near a beaver's dam on the other side of the river.

Jimmy caught nine fish, which now lay stiff in the snow. He was ready to carry them up to Old Mother's tipi when a girl, taller than he and quite large, pointed to his pole.

"Can I use that?" she asked.

He thought a moment. He had noticed the beautiful Nahanee on the bank behind him, wrapped in a fur robe. He was sure she was watching.

"All right," he told the girl, trying to appear generous. "But I will need it again."

When Jimmy returned later, the girl had several fish in a basket by her side. She was standing over the hole and she didn't look at him.

"Hello," Jimmy said. "I need my pole."

"No."

"What?" He had been pleasant enough. Why wouldn't she give it back?

"A *tybo* in fancy Indian clothes does not need to fish."

"Please, it's mine!" He reached for the pole but she jerked it away, then smacked him over the head with it, knocking him to his knees.

Jimmy slipped on the ice as he struggled to his feet. He knew he should be nice to girls, but this one was big and she was mean. He shoved her down. Before she could get up, he yanked her braid until she spun on her back.

She screamed. Her voice echoed across the ice like ten girls screaming and now Jimmy knew there would be trouble.

He ran for the lodge. As soon as he ducked inside, a squaw pushed her way past Old Mother, a knife in her hand.

"Give me that *tybo* in show-off clothes," she hissed. "I will cut his heart out." She lunged for him but Old Mother tripped her, then grabbed the woman's ankles and dragged her out to the snow.

By now the noise had drawn the rest of the camp. The girl's mother slapped Old Mother across the cheek then reached for a chunk of firewood protruding from the snow.

Jimmy was scared. He didn't know women fought like men. The mother was raising the wood over Old Mother's head. Jimmy leapt on her arm and wrestled her to the ground.

"Leave my mother alone!" he yelled.

Another woman grabbed the mother around the waist and pushed her face in the snow. Immediately others took sides and jumped in, fighting and squalling.

Jimmy held the club, ready to swing if anyone lunged for Old Mother.

When Hanabi pulled the club from his hands, he rushed into the tipi for his bow. He was hooking an arrow when a stooped figure in the doorway stopped him. Mozo the elder gently took the bow away. He looked at Jimmy.

Jimmy backed up and sat on a pile of robes. He felt ashamed.

Outside the ruckus stopped. Nampa and another brave had separated the fighters.

Before sundown, Washakie returned from his hunt. When he learned what had happened in his absence, he held a council in the big tipi. The next morning, three families packed their *travois* and left to join another band. The chief would tolerate no threats to his family.

That's the last girl I'll ever talk to, Jimmy promised himself.

13

Squaw Boy

Spring soon warmed the hills. The river flowed with ice as chunks broke away from shore.

Jimmy thought about his family. *Has baby Lucy survived her first winter?* For once he wished he could hear his sisters argue. *I wish there was a way to tell Mother I am all right.*

Remembering her, he looked at Old Mother. She was like an eagle with a wing spread over her chick. Jimmy hurried to gather wood for her, then down to the river for water. Every day he would help her, he decided. Enough for two mothers. Then maybe he wouldn't miss his own so much.

The other boys teased him. "Squaw boy!" they called. "You are doing squaw's work."

"They're making me mad," Jimmy told Old Mother.

"Leave them, Dawii. They are bad boys."

But one morning Jimmy had cut more wood than he could carry at one time. When he returned for the second load, Poog stepped out from behind a tree. He spat at Jimmy's feet.

"Ssssquaw," he hissed. Then he spat in Jimmy's face.

Jimmy dropped the wood, pulled his ax from his belt, and chased after him. Washakie saw the boys.

"Dawii!"

Jimmy stopped. Poog fled to the safety of his lodge.

"What is this about?"

Jimmy told him, trying not to cry in frustration.

"I do not want you to start another camp brawl, but I do want you to defend yourself," Washakie said. "My young warriors will never leave you alone if they think you are a coward. However, they respect one who can walk away from trouble. Without wood, the fire goes out."

Jimmy looked up at Washakie's face and relaxed when he saw the kindness in his eyes.

"I've been watching," the chief said. "I am pleased to see that you're not starting these fights. I believe you are a peaceful one if left alone.

"Dawii, you have protected our mother," he said, referring to the brawl over the fishing pole. He placed his hands on Jimmy's shoulders. "I am proud we are brothers."

One evening, after things had quieted down with Poog, Jimmy sat inside the large tipi, playing with Oddo, who was crawling around the soft furs. Washakie stood outside watching stars. Jimmy heard footsteps crunch in the snow, then a man complain to the chief.

"This white boy is showing Indian boys bad things. He should not be doing women's work. He is trying to change our ways. You should not let him, Washakie."

The chief laughed. "Dawii wants to please our mother. It does not hurt for us to help each other.

"Since Dawii came, she has seen many good moons. He is so much comfort to her that now I know if he hadn't come to us, grief would have killed her."

Jimmy listened. What he heard next made him ache for Old Mother. It also filled him with despair because it suddenly occurred to him that his own mother might be grieving as well.

14

Avalanche

When Jimmy heard Washakie invite the man into the tipi, he quickly wrapped himself in a robe, pretending sleep. He did not want to see a critical face. Hanabi seemed to understand, for she tended Oddo as if Jimmy had been asleep all along.

Washakie sat first in front of the fire on the north side of the lodge, then the other Indian sat an arm's reach away. Jimmy knew the silence meant Washakie was lighting his long-stemmed pipe to share with the visitor. It meant he was about to tell a story, as true and straight as the pipe.

"Before you joined our band," Washakie told the man, his voice calm, "I had a small sister named Yati. She was seven winters when she fell from her pony and was dragged to her death. The day after Yati died, fighting broke out again among the Crow and Shoshoni.

"My father was wounded in the arm with a poisoned arrow. He lived for two suns after the battle. Old Mother cut her hair and her fingers to show her grief for her daughter and husband."

Now Jimmy understood why Old Mother's braids weren't as long as Hanabi's, and why the fingertips on her left hand were missing.

"Her wounds of grief had not yet healed," Washakie continued, "when my two younger brothers, Nuva and Posena, went hunting mountain sheep during the snows. They were climbing a steep hill that faced the sun. The snow gave way."

Washakie refilled his pipe with a small clump of *kinnikinnick* and lit it. He passed it to his visitor.

"My young brothers were swept into a deep gorge. When they did not return by sundown, we began searching. We found the trail of the snow river and we hurried to the bottom of the canyon. We poked long sticks into the snow, but we couldn't find my brothers."

Jimmy dared a peek from under an edge of his robe, turning as if in his sleep. Hanabi was on the opposite side of the lodge, diapering Oddo with wads of cattail down and bundling her up for the night. He could see Washakie's arm as it raised and passed the pipe. An eagle feather dangled from its stem, which was wrapped with strips of yellow horsehair.

Jimmy grew sleepy from the warmth of the fire

and the lateness of the evening, but he was not going to miss Washakie's story, even though he dreaded to hear its end. He wasn't sure he wanted to know the depth of Old Mother's sorrow.

Washakie paused several minutes before continuing. He added some buffalo chips to the fire. It cracked and sizzled, casting deep shadows against the sides of the lodge.

"My mother went every day to dig with a stick," he continued. "But she became so ill with grief and from lying in the snow, I had to carry her back to our lodge. She lay near death for two moons. As soon as she could walk, she returned to digging."

Jimmy listened from inside his robe. He could hear Oddo nursing loudly at Hanabi's breast and the slight rustle of the pipe being passed. Several minutes went by before Washakie spoke.

"When Old Mother came to the canyon, she saw the legs of my brother, Nuva, sticking out of the melting snow. Wolves had eaten his feet. With her hands she dug up his body. She kept digging until she found Posena. This was a terrible thing for a mother to discover. Since she was too weak to return to our village, and she didn't want to leave my brothers to the wolves, she stayed."

The chief's voice was still low and even, but Jimmy thought he heard a catch—a sigh, perhaps, that stopped in the throat. Washakie paused to compose himself.

"Mozo and I found her at daybreak," he continued. "She was lying in the snow. Her arms were over the bodies of my brothers. I put her in a *travois* and returned to camp. Mozo sat near my brothers until others could come help.

"For many moons Old Mother was ill. Nothing would comfort her. She slept most of the time, and while she slept she dreamed a wonderful dream. In this dream, she was happy because she had a new son. This child was a white boy."

When Jimmy heard this, his heart thumped inside his chest. Old Mother had been expecting him as surely as if he were a guest arriving for Christmas dinner.

"We were near the big *tybo* village," Washakie said. "When our scouts saw Dawii playing by himself every day, they wanted to steal him for Old Mother.

"I said, 'No, do not force him.' I said if the boy wants to come, then bring him."

All this time, Washakie's visitor listened. *Why doesn't he ask questions?* Jimmy wondered. There was so much Jimmy wanted to know, he could have interrupted dozens of times. Now Jimmy was beginning to understand why Old Mother cherished him and why she hated to let him out of her sight. He felt proud to be so important, yet he was nervous about the responsibility it brought.

What if I return to my own family? What would happen to Old Mother?

Washakie turned the bowl of his pipe upside down and laid it next to the fire. The story was over. The guest stood to leave.

"I believe the Great Spirit sent Dawii to my mother."

15

Horse Thieves

Wild lupine, syringa, and mountain daisies bloomed between patches of snow. The air was cool and filled with the sounds of woodpeckers high in the trees and squirrels chasing each other among the branches.

Jimmy was helping Old Mother take down their lodge poles when a cry rang out. Fifty horses were missing, stolen in the night by Crow.

Ga-mu raced up to Jimmy, out of breath, his braids swinging at his waist. "They were Washakie's best ponies. Let's go!"

Old Mother put her hand on Jimmy's arm. He wanted to ride off with the others and return a hero. But he looked at her amputated fingers and remembered her lost children.

Ga-mu seemed to understand. With a jump, he was on his horse and off.

Pinto Bean was staked safely nearby. Jimmy

stroked the velvet end of her nose. How he wished he could sneak away for some adventure.

It was the way of life, he'd noticed. The Crow tribe would steal horses from the Shoshoni, Shoshoni would steal them back plus some extra for good measure, then the Crow would return for another raid. Back and forth.

If they met face-to-face, there would be some fighting and whooping, sometimes they'd scalp one another, then there'd be a big dance. Jimmy wished they could settle things once and for all. But he had learned that Indians valued horses more than white people valued gold. To lose a horse was to lose a trusted companion.

When the sun was overhead, Ga-mu and Nampa returned with the others. They had followed the Crow trail over a crest and into a valley, but the horses were too many hours ahead. This they could tell from the droppings, which had frozen in the night and which were spread out from the running.

Camp was moved south. After two days they met another large group of Shoshoni and traveled together for four days until they found plains rich with elk, *bojono*, deer, and antelope. Here the tribe could dig for roots under the blue camas flower. Onions topped with pink blossoms were plentiful, as was wild parsley, the roots of which could be ground into meal for biscuits.

Within an hour of stopping, the women had raised the lodges near the shores of a sparkling lake. Forty years earlier the white explorer Major Andrew Henry was so pleased to have discovered this lake that he named it after himself. Henry's Lake was where Washakie's band would spend part of the summer, as generations before them had.

Jimmy spent his days fishing and playing with Nampa and Ga-mu, who, while old enough to hunt with the men, were just as happy playing near camp. Both were taller than Jimmy, lean, and dark-skinned. Jimmy, too, was tanned now and his brown hair was turning lighter with each day outdoors.

The boys were always on the lookout for Poog and—Jimmy hoped this secretly—Nahanee. He liked showing off when he thought she was watching.

One afternoon after Jimmy had been running antelope, Washakie met him at the edge of camp.

"You are working your pony too hard, Dawii."

Pinto Bean was thinner. Jimmy followed Washakie to a field where other horses grazed.

"Let her rest and get fat with the others. I have something to show you."

Washakie helped Jimmy up onto his horse and

together they rode to a grove of cottonwoods alongside a wide stream. Several boys with ropes were
trying to calm bucking colts.

The chief and Jimmy slid to the ground and
walked over to a pretty roan. She was stocky like
the other Indian ponies, and stepping high with
spirit.

"For me?" Jimmy was wide-eyed, exhilarated.
He tried to put his face against the horse's square
jaw, but it jerked back to the end of its tether.

"She is still wild, but not as wild as the colts.
If you can ride her, she's yours."

Jimmy reached to pet her again. "Easy, girl,
shh." He had assumed all horses were as gentle as
Pinto Bean. Now he had something new to think
about, something *thrilling* to think about.

Washakie handed him the reins, which were the
ends of a long rope that was looped and knotted
around the horse's lower jaw to form a simple bit.
When Washakie nodded toward the stream, Jimmy
untied his moccasins and put them under a tree.
He might be in for a wet ride.

They waded out to the center of the stream where
the current came up to the roan's belly. The water
felt icy around Jimmy's chest and it numbed his
feet; he shivered with cold and excitement. He could
see clearly down to the sandy bottom littered with

colored stones. Even though there were goose bumps all up and down his legs, Jimmy wasn't about to complain. The Indian boys were diving and splashing one another as if they were in a warm bath.

Washakie put his hand under Jimmy's elbow and floated him up to where he could easily slide a leg over the horse's side and settle himself on her back. Jimmy held the reins, threading his fingers through the long reddish strands of her mane. Then he took a deep breath.

"All right, Red," he said. He leaned forward, squeezed his legs against her sides, and flashed a nervous look at Washakie, who stood to the side grinning. Jimmy was proud that the chief trusted him with such a task.

Washakie slapped the roan's rump. She stretched her neck forward, trying to swim to shore. Before she reached the sandbar, Washakie grabbed the reins and led her back into the middle of the stream.

Every time she tried to rear up, the water prevented a kick and helped Jimmy to keep his balance. The next day he returned, and each day afterward he rode her in shallower waters.

Jimmy loved the feel of Red's strong muscles below him and how she stomped impatiently while he held the reins tight. Finally, he loosened his hold and she burst forward into a gallop.

Her mane flew back, stinging Jimmy's face. Her tail streamed behind. Soon other boys on their ponies were racing alongside them, *yeee-ipping* with the exhilaration of speed. The pounding hooves shook the earth. The sun-dried prairie sped by in a blur. Jimmy's eyes watered, his mouth open in a happy yell.

Riders approached from ahead, slowing the boys' horses. They were hunters with a frantic message: Crow were riding their way, fast, painted for war.

16

Lost

The camp was in an uproar. It seemed that everyone ran around and talked at the same time. It reminded Jimmy of Brigham Young's fort when he was just eight, and how the settlers were in constant fear of Indian attacks.

The sounds of children crying and of mothers hushing them were the same. The sounds of men shouting instructions were the same. Jimmy closed his eyes. The sounds of horses pacing and snorting were the same. The smell of dust in the air, the feeling of fear; it was all the same.

Warriors were smearing black paint, made of charcoal and bear grease, on their foreheads and around their eyes. Jimmy watched as they mixed a palm full of grease with pollen and dried berries to draw yellow and red stripes on their cheeks. The boys rounded up the fastest horses and took them among the tipis to await riders.

Washakie sat high in his saddle, from which dangled stirrups of soft beaded leather. His war-bonnet had two trails of feathers flowing down his back and the brow band was beaded with dark blue and white triangles. His grayish hair spread over his shoulders like a magnificent mane. His lance pointed toward the clouds.

Chief Washakie gave one yell and raised his staff. With a slight press of his moccasin, his horse bolted forward, flanked by ready warriors.

Jimmy raced to where Pinto Bean and Red were staked. Old Mother hurried after him.

"They need me," Jimmy called back to her. "I've gotta help fight!"

"I will tell you when to fight," she said, catching up to him. "You stay by me. It would take you five suns on your pony to get a Crow," she said, hoping to discourage him. She lifted his hand and pressed it against her heart.

"Dawii, you have scared me too many times."

With the warriors gone, the camp was quiet. Children played along the river and a group of boys on horseback chased antelope.

The next morning, Mozo rode with Jimmy into the forested foothills to hunt elk. After two hours, they saw a small herd in a clearing, grazing on the yellow flowers of the bitterbrush. The old man motioned to Jimmy and they slid to the soft, pine-scented ground, where they lay on their bellies.

Mozo drew an arrow and pulled his arm back. A large cow elk jerked sideways when the arrow hit, ran a few yards, then fell.

"Shoot her in the neck, Dawii," he said. "Then slit her throat to bleed her and wait until I return." Before Jimmy could protest, Mozo crept after a buck that was headed toward a canyon.

Why did Mozo have to leave? Jimmy was already nervous from the war preparations of the day before and now Mozo had left him alone. *What if the Crow decide to sneak up?*

Jimmy stepped cautiously toward the fallen cow. He'd heard stories about wounded animals playing dead then attacking the approaching hunter. Jimmy wasn't taking any chances. He fired his own eight arrows into her, plus a dozen more Ga-mu had given him.

The elk didn't move. Jimmy threw sticks at it. He sat against a rock and waited. Much later, when it still hadn't moved, he felt it was safe to check the huge animal. He pulled his knife from his belt and drew it across the elk's throat. Not a drop of blood came out.

Jimmy had waited too long. Now the animal would rot quickly lying on the moist ground.

Jimmy looked about for Mozo. He called, he whistled. He didn't quite remember the way back to camp, but he started walking anyway. Moss grew on the north side of logs, he knew that. He looked up at the sky. He knew that the tips of fir trees leaned south, toward the sun, and that the branches were more numerous facing south. But whether camp was south or west or north or east, he could not remember. Mozo had told him to memorize their trail, but Jimmy, uneasy about Washakie being at war, hadn't paid attention.

As he wandered, he grew more and more frightened. The horses weren't where he'd thought they were and when he retraced his steps, the dead elk was gone. There was a stream where he hadn't seen one before.

"Mozo?" he cried, louder this time. "Mozo?" He whistled and whistled, hoping Pinto Bean would hear. Jimmy sat down on a rock. He rested his chin on his knees and closed his eyes in despair.

Waazip. He was lost.

The more Jimmy realized how alone he was, the more worried he became. *What has happened to Mozo?* he wondered. *Could he have been ambushed? Is he hurt?*

Jimmy didn't know how to begin searching for the elder. Besides, he was hungry. It was getting cold. His moccasins were damp and somehow he'd ripped his shirt. A mountain lion could come after him, or a bear, or *three* bears.

In a flash he climbed a tree, clinging nervously to a thick branch oozing with sap. He might be sticky, but at least the bears couldn't get him, he thought with relief. Jimmy had forgotten how much young bears and mountain lions enjoy climbing trees.

Hours passed. A crescent moon rose in the black sky. An owl hooted, another answered. Jimmy shivered with cold. Every rustle sounded like a grizzly coming near. He listened to crickets chirping and felt sure that enemy Crow were signaling one another. The owls began hooting with more frequency.

The sounds of the forest grew louder as the minutes passed.

Suddenly a line of horses trampled nearby and Jimmy's heart pounded in his throat. *Crow!* He was close to panic.

But a familiar voice cried out.

"Dawii!"

Jimmy opened his mouth to yell, but his tongue was so dry no sound came.

"Dawii!" the voice called again in the darkness.

Soon the brush below his tree cracked and Jimmy saw the dim form of Washakie.

"I'm up h-h-here," Jimmy whimpered.

"Why are you up there?"

Jimmy was shivering so much it was hard to talk. "I-I can't find my horse," he managed.

"Your horse is not up there."

"I know."

"Come down, Dawii. The whole tribe is searching for you. Old Mother is crazy with worry. It would be better for us if some Indian would kill you so we could get some sleep. I have a thought to do it myself."

Jimmy rode behind Washakie—his arms around the chief's waist, his face against his back—drinking in the comforting, smoky smell from Washakie's buckskin shirt. He was happy the chief had returned safely from the Crow skirmish and relieved that he soon would be home.

When they reached the clearing, Washakie hallooed to let everyone know Dawii was safe. Indians yelled back from the timber.

Old Mother ran from her tipi scolding and crying when she saw Jimmy.

"You did not listen to Mozo. I thought a big bear ate you."

"He just said to wait, he didn't say for how long," Jimmy said.

"Ai!" She waved her hand in front of her. In the firelight Jimmy saw the years in her face. "He told you to wait. You did not wait. When he returned for you, you had already made plans of your own . . . *waazip!* Have you lived so long that you know more than your elders?"

The next morning Jimmy and Mozo returned for the elk even though it had begun to rot. Jimmy brought it to Old Mother and proudly showed it off.

"I'll make you moccasins from the hide, Old Mother."

"You are a good son, Dawii, but the skin is spoiled."

"It'll wash out good. I can do it."

"Yes, Little Hunter, I know you can. But how will you fill those holes from your twenty arrows?"

1 7

Questions for a Chief

Nampa and Ga-mu sat with Jimmy on a boulder in the stream. A small waterfall trickled below their feet into a clear, deep pool.

"We came to the *Sogwobipa*," Nampa began. "Crow were on the other side." Jimmy knew they were talking about the head of the Missouri River.

"We waited until dark. We went in for their ponies and got thirty-two to run with us, but the Crow were awake. Their arrows killed our cousin and crippled my horse."

Nampa had jumped on the dead man's horse and broken away with the others. They were chased for hours. More arrows and wounded horses.

Jimmy swished his bare foot in the water. He had listened to their story, now he was thinking.

"You traded thirty-two horses for the life of your cousin."

"It's not fair," Jimmy said to Washakie. They were walking in the moonlight toward their lodge.

"You are right, Dawii," he said. "It's not fair, but the Crow would have done the same to us."

"You're the chief. Can't you make peace?"

"When you are grown, Dawii, you can change things your way. It isn't as easy as you think." They stood outside the tipis. Sounds of families settling down for the night could be heard. An old woman's voice sang softly.

"There should be peace," Washakie said after several moments. "The Great Spirit does not like fighting among brothers."

"Then why do people fight?"

"This I can't answer."

Jimmy tried to think of something to say. He wanted to feel safe and he wanted to believe that his own family was safe. "Do Shoshoni hate white people as much as they hate Crow?"

Washakie looked at him, remembering his first meeting with whites fifty years earlier. Lewis and Clark had come to the Shoshoni in peace and the Shoshoni had promised peace in return. Washakie was loyal to that memory. "I will never fight *tybo*. A warrior who attacks a *tybo* is not from Chief Washakie. I forbid our people to fight with the settlers."

"But you will fight other Indians?"

"When I was a young man, Dawii, I enjoyed war. Even when our tribe was at peace, I wandered off, looking for trouble, looking for enemies. I am sad to tell you that I killed many Indians. For this reason I'm ashamed to speak of my youth."

Jimmy was still confused. He'd never worried much about what people did or what they felt, but for some reason he now cared deeply. This new emotion made him bold.

"No one wins if everyone keeps fighting," Jimmy said as carefully as possible. "Maybe if the chiefs put their pipes together they can agree to stop once and for all. You don't have to like each other. You just have to all want peace." It was the longest speech Jimmy had ever made.

Washakie slowly lifted his face to the stars.

1 8

Nahanee

Once again lodge covers were folded onto *travois* and a slow journey was begun. Washakie's band headed for open country, traveling south for seven days along the *Piupa*, through the valley that one day would be named Jackson Hole. Jimmy tried to count all the Indians stretching ahead of him and behind him, but there were too many.

To the west, the Tetons, their crags white with snow even in the summer, towered over a string of lakes. The surrounding grasslands were spotted with stands of pine and aspen. A black bear and her cubs meandered through a marsh bordered by huckleberry shrubs.

Where the *Piupa* eased west, the women raised tipis and lit cooking fires. The river was narrow but deep enough for diving, which was what most of the boys began doing.

Jimmy was pleased to notice Nahanee watching

him from her mother's lodge. He fancied himself quite a swimmer and this was a perfect chance to show off his diving skills.

With a flourish, he stretched his arms into an arc and tilted his chin toward the sky. He bent his knees and sprang, launching himself into the river. The sudden slap of his skin on the surface knocked the breath out of him, bringing giggles from the audience. Jimmy came up gasping. He had done a spectacular bellyflop.

Thunder rumbled through the darkening clouds. Steam rose from the warm earth as raindrops fell, releasing the fragrant smell of sagebrush. Jimmy sat inside the lodge with Hanabi and baby Oddo. Old Mother stirred fresh yamps into a pot simmering over the fire. Jimmy enjoyed the sound of rain against the tent.

By afternoon the sun was out and the earth felt clean and fresh. Jimmy wandered around camp. It fit Old Mother's requirements: good grass, good wood, good water. When he looked back at his tipi, he noticed that it stood on the northeast side of a cottonwood tree. Jimmy marveled at the precise way Old Mother had raised their lodge. It was just out of reach of the dripping leaves, yet close enough for shade and protection from the wind.

Like the other tipis in camp, it was squat, about twelve feet high, and the doorway opened to the morning light. Old Mother often explained why. "The Creator gives us the sun to make us warm and to make all things grow. This is the first thing we see after our sleep. We give thanks for each new sun."

Jimmy followed a trail along the river. A family of raccoons was on the bank, dipping paws in the water. He sat on a mossy log to watch. The mother raccoon hooked a crayfish and flung it onto the muddy bank, where her three kits examined it, then batted it playfully.

Something stirred in the ferns. Jimmy listened. Without moving his head, he turned his eyes toward the sound.

The noise was not that of a small animal, he could tell. It didn't scurry off and its movements were slow and deliberate. He waited.

Minutes passed. The bush rustled again and out stepped Nahanee. She looked down at her moccasins.

"Hello, Dawii." A blush spread over her cheeks.

"Hi." He was surprised she was alone, as the women and girls customarily stayed in pairs. Jimmy had never been this close to her. She was more beautiful than he'd realized. She looked soft. He wanted to touch the sleeve of her deerskin dress where a row of blue and white beads had been stitched by her mother.

She sat down beside him. Jimmy thought she smelled of clean, warm skin and campfire smoke. It was nice. He pretended to study the raccoons.

"Wanna swim?" he asked, uneasy with the nearness of her. But then he remembered his bellyflop and he felt the heat rise in his face. Every time he tried to show off for Nahanee, it didn't work.

"Or we could throw rocks," he said quickly. "Bet you can't get one all the way across."

She smiled at him. "We don't have to do anything, Dawii. It is nice just sitting here." Her dark eyes matched her hair, which was braided neatly over her shoulders, each end wrapped in a strip of buckskin. Her hair was shiny with the bear grease all the women used.

Now Jimmy didn't know what to say. He'd never had trouble talking to his sisters—except maybe Rose, who was only two, and Clara, bossy Clara.

But this was different. There was a flutter in his stomach when he looked at Nahanee. He wanted to show off, to do something so she would like him.

"Let's walk," she said, standing. "I know a place. It is quiet and high and we can see the eagles nesting."

As Jimmy followed Nahanee uphill along the river, he noticed how her dress swayed and how her moccasins pressed softly on the trail. Sunlight filtered through the branches, bringing alive the scent of balsam and soil and Nahanee. He touched her arm. When she turned to him, he was overwhelmed with a desire he couldn't understand.

As he stared at her, she started walking again. Soon the trail leveled and widened into a clearing. She stopped.

Below, the river snaked its way through the valley. Nahanee pointed to what looked like a large ragged basket nestled in the top of a tree. Barely visible were the heads of two small birds, beaks pointed upward.

Jimmy and Nahanee sat in the afternoon sun, watching, listening. She peeled a pinecone, then shared *deeba*, the tasty nuts, with Jimmy.

"*Kreeee,*" a cry sounded from the sky. "*Kreee . . . kreee.*" An eagle circled nearby, gliding toward her nest. Jimmy was close enough to see that her wingspan was wider than he was tall. Her head was white. Clutched in her talons, which were as big as Jimmy's hands, was a limp brown rabbit.

For another hour they watched the eagle in the nest. Then she balanced herself on the rim, pumped her great wings, and rose in flight over the valley.

Jimmy was filled with awe. Nothing matched the grandeur of this eagle. He looked at Nahanee. Her face showed the same wonder he felt. He inched his hand toward her hand and when they touched, she turned to him with a smile.

For once Jimmy had no desire to show off.

19

Another Fight

One warm afternoon Jimmy was breaking a colt while several younger boys ran in the shallow stream alongside him. Jimmy was whooping with fun until he saw the figure behind a tree.

It was Poog, and he held a long stick. When the colt bucked by, Poog jabbed at its side.

"Hey you!" Jimmy yelled. "Cut it out!"

"I want you to fall, *tybo*. For that kick you gave me!"

Jimmy raced the colt around some brush. *He has a grudge, but I don't wanna fight him.* He remembered the eagle. It symbolized everything he wanted to be: it was calm, strong, and it was treated with respect.

By the time Jimmy noticed Poog had closed in, it was too late. Smack! went the stick against the colt's forelegs. The young horse reared.

"I'm warning you, Poog. Leave us be." Jimmy tried to ride away, but Poog followed.

Smack! again.

A long rawhide rope was tied to the colt's halter. Jimmy made a noose from the rope and held it between his fingers. Meanwhile, he tried to widen the distance between him and Poog.

But Poog managed to jab the horse's ribs once again. Jimmy twirled the rope and aimed the noose for Poog's shoulders. Instead, it landed around Poog's neck and jerked him off his feet.

The colt was startled into a run. Before Jimmy could stop him, Poog had been dragged several yards through the dirt. Blood spilled from his nose and mouth.

Jimmy jumped down and quickly loosened the noose. Poog opened his eyes and squalled.

"I'm sorry, brother," Jimmy tried. But Poog was already running back to camp, screaming. Jimmy followed.

Old Mother met him. "Dawii, what have you done now?"

"Almost killed him, but I didn't mean to." Jimmy's shoulders fell in despair. "He wouldn't leave me alone. I'm sorry I hurt him, I really am."

"There is going to be another camp fight over this," Old Mother said. Several Indians walked their way. When Jimmy saw Poog's mother and father marching over, he ran for Pinto Bean.

"I don't wanna fight. It's not my fault!" he cried as he grabbed the pony's mane and swung up. He galloped bareback several miles downriver, then hid in a cave of willows. He was mad at himself for running away, but he didn't know how to be brave all the time.

Near sundown, he heard voices in the distance calling, "Dawii! Dawii!" It seemed odd to Jimmy that they hadn't found him yet, for he knew they certainly could if they wanted to.

Mosquitoes swarmed around his eyes and mouth, biting his cheeks and bare arms. He crept away from the riverbrush and sat on a stump where he was sure no one could see him. Near a pile of driftwood, he poked a sharp stick in the dirt until he found a mouse hole. Inside was a nest of camas roots, the bulbs as big and white as his thumbnail. Jimmy chewed on them, enjoying their potatolike taste, even though they would have been better cooked. He drank some water to ease his hunger.

If it weren't for Old Mother, he would never go back. Now he longed more than ever for his people on the Great Salt Lake. He wasn't sorry about Poog, mean Poog. But he hadn't hurt him on purpose. As Jimmy brooded, he realized he was a stranger in two worlds and he had stirred up the biggest mess imaginable.

He had brought heartache upon two mothers.

As the moon rose, he decided to return. "Humility comes before honor," he reasoned, remembering his father's words. How he missed his father now! He was embarrassed to face his Indian family.

Jimmy walked Pinto Bean toward camp. In the distance he saw riders heading his way.

2 0

Lecture

"Dawii!" Nampa and Ga-mu called. When they saw
how slowly Jimmy was walking, they laughed. "No
one is going to hurt you. You were defending yourself."

Jimmy felt better. As they rode into camp, Washakie approached them. Light from the campfire
played against the side of his face. Jimmy tried not
to stare at the deep scar below the chief's cheek-
bone.

"Never run off like that again, Dawii."

"I was afraid of a big fight."

"Come to me next time. There is only more
trouble when you run from a problem."

Jimmy explained how Poog and he had tangled.

"A boy tied to a wild horse does not make much
fun for the boy," Washakie said.

"It happened so fast and I was so mad, I didn't
think about it."

"Always think, Dawii."

Jimmy rubbed the toe of his moccasin in the dirt.

"Poog's neck is scraped raw. He could have died. His parents are very upset."

Serves him right, thought Jimmy. He was still mad but when he saw Poog moping through camp, Jimmy felt sorry. He gave him a half-smile, but Poog sneered and turned away.

In the tipi that night Jimmy lay in his robe, exhausted. Washakie visited with Old Mother. They talked, thinking he slept.

"Maybe Dawii isn't happy with us," Old Mother said. Her hands worked quietly over a new pair of moccasins as she spoke. "When he ran away from camp, I know he must have thought of his other family. I know his white mother thinks about him."

Washakie let the sound of the fire fill the silence. He looked at Jimmy's sandy hair and felt a rush of tenderness. They were brothers.

Jimmy began to doze. He had avoided thinking about how his white family might feel. But Old Mother's words filled him with longing.

He pictured the cottage, how his mother was up before everyone else, before dawn, working in candlelight. Since it was Jimmy's only chance to be alone with her, he would often rise early just to sit near her, sleepily stirring the batter for hotcakes or filling the cast-iron muffin pans. By the time Father awakened, loaves of bread would be baking in the iron stove, Mother would be nursing baby Lucy, and Molly would be setting breakfast on the long oak table, the aroma of fresh coffee filling the room. Clara would pour milk from a pail into the blue pitcher.

Jimmy pictured nightfall. His sisters would clear the supper table while Mother rocked Lucy's cradle with her foot and held Annie and Rose on her lap for lullabies. Emma and Frances would be jumping on their corn-husk mattress and Nan would be stitching by firelight.

Jimmy would fetch water and wood for morning, then do his reading lessons. By the time they rolled into bed, Father would already be snoring in the four-poster while Mother washed the dishes and pots. She didn't use soap—that way, at dawn, the dish-water could be fed to the hogs.

Then she would blow out the last candle.

Old Mother and Washakie sat by the fire, still not speaking. Jimmy wanted to sleep now, but there was one last picture in his mind.

His sister Olivia. He remembered how excited

she had been to marry Thomas Messersmith and start her own family. He remembered the horrible day Olivia died, just a few hours after giving birth to her first baby. She had been seventeen.

Jimmy shuddered at that memory. A sharp stab of guilt made him sob into the fur. His mother had lost Olivia. He hadn't really considered her grief. And now she'd lost him, too.

21

The Eagle

Mosquitos were so bothersome along *Piupa*, Washakie's band traveled through a westward canyon to the eastern foothills of the Tetons. For the hot month of August they camped near a stream rippling with trout and banked with willows. Moose grazed in the soggy meadows nearby.

Jimmy continued to pretend that he was president of the Jimmy Spoon Club and that his unknowing friends were members. He liked hunting with Nampa and Ga-mu. One morning, their arrows brought down seven white-tailed deer.

"Now I shall sew you warm clothes," Old Mother told him when he brought her some hides. "In two moons there will be snows."

Even though the weeks passed peacefully, scouts were always watching. Sometimes the wind played tricks by blowing dust, making it appear that enemies were approaching.

Washakie rode with Jimmy through the valley.

"When I was ten winters, the Shoshoni and Sioux fought here. So many were killed. So many." Washakie sat tall on his horse as he surveyed the basin. A breeze blew wisps of gray hair around his face.

"Are we staying here for the winter?" Jimmy asked.

"The snows will be too deep, Dawii. When the *bojono* are fat, we'll take the meat we need and follow the antelope." He pointed west. A smile lifted the chief's face. "There are fish there that measure as long as you. They swim upstream instead of down."

Jimmy felt like a real Indian now that his hair was long enough to braid. Old Mother gave him thin strips of red wool edged in white to wrap around each end. When Washakie told him he was ready for an eagle feather, Jimmy was thrilled but also worried. He had seen the sharp talons and mighty wings. Would he have to catch it himself?

"The eagle carries messages from the Great Spirit. Because of this, its feathers are sacred. We are close to our Creator when we greet each sun with prayer, when we end each sun with prayer, and when we wear the feather of our brother, Eagle." Washakie looked at Jimmy with affection.

"It is a great honor to take a feather without harming the bird. You are ready for such an honor, Dawii."

Before the next sunrise, Nampa and Ga-mu rode with Jimmy into the foothills, a buffalo robe tied behind each saddle, a bow and quiver each. When they reached a plateau, Nampa stopped. High above they could hear the familiar cry.

"Kreeee . . ."

"Long ago, our grandfathers were friends with the Teton Sioux," Nampa said. "They learned the Sioux way of catching an eagle."

Both Nampa and Ga-mu had a narrow braid at each temple, adorned with beads and brass tubing. Their pompadours were greased into a thicker braid that lay down their backs. Jimmy's hair fell loose below his shoulders. They dismounted and led their horses to a shallow stream.

Jimmy followed the boys' directions and began digging in the soft earth with his hands. When there was a pit large enough for him to crouch in, he stopped.

"Now, fresh meat." Nampa said no more.

The sun was hot against Jimmy's back as he hunted, his shirt tied around his waist. His arrows hit a young mule deer that had paused at the edge of a pond to drink.

Ga-mu nodded his approval when Jimmy returned and began cutting away the hide. He showed Jimmy how to line the pit with his buffalo robe, then how to sit, knees up and arms ready. Then Nampa spread branches over the top, leaving an opening in the center small enough for Jimmy's hand. Onto the branches he dropped a chunk of raw deer meat.

"Do not sleep, Dawii."

Jimmy was alone. It was cool in the pit. He could smell the meat and hear the flies buzzing in the sun.

It grew dark. He ate some serviceberries from the pouch looped over his belt. As the hours passed, Jimmy became drowsy. He sat as straight as he could without bumping the camouflage above him, but still he had trouble staying awake. He wanted to stretch out, to relieve himself. Oh, to sleep! How he wanted to close his eyes for just a minute.

Getting an eagle feather now seemed silly. Maybe he should earn his feather by touching an enemy instead. He hadn't felt so miserable since his raw legs more than a year ago. He gazed up through a crack in the branches at a black sky pricked with stars. Every time he started to count them, his eyes grew heavy and his head dropped to his shoulder.

Then it was dawn. Had he slept? Had he missed the bird? He felt for the meat and was heartened when he found it still there, frigid from the cold night.

As the sun rose in the sky, Jimmy yearned to climb from the hole. Every muscle in his back, legs, and neck ached to be stretched.

Finally, he heard the cry, muffled at first, but coming closer. Jimmy's heart pounded as he tried to remember everything the boys had told him. There would be one chance. One chance only.

A shadow swooped overhead. Slowly Jimmy raised his hands, ready. A thud above scattered loose twigs onto his face, but he shook them away. The eagle had landed on the meat.

Jimmy thrust his right hand under the bird, fingers splayed so he could grab the legs. The bird jumped, but Jimmy held tight. With his left hand he reached high to grab the scruff of its neck. More branches fell on him as the bird struggled fiercely.

Jimmy's heart raced. His breath came in gasps. The eagle was even bigger than he'd expected and so strong that Jimmy's arms ached. It tried to lift its wings.

Now.

Jimmy opened his mouth and bit down on the tip of a tail feather. It felt slippery between his teeth, but he clenched them tight. Gently, Jimmy pulled his head back until he felt a small pluck. The feather was out. He opened his hands and the bird flew free.

Nampa stepped out from the trees with a smile so broad Jimmy knew he had done it right. Ga-mu motioned in a graceful arc, signifying *Well done.* The backs of Jimmy's hands were bleeding, but he felt no pain.

He had a feather. And he had taken it without killing the bird.

2 2

Grizzly

Washakie's hunters had shot a great number of moose, elk, and deer in preparation for the coming fall. Women worked into the night, drying meat and tanning hides until everything could be packed for travel. Then they were up before dawn with the children to gather berries.

Jimmy loved working between Old Mother and Hanabi, filling baskets with raspberries and serviceberries. They would spread blankets beneath the branches and shake the trees as hard as they could. The children had fun beating sticks against the branches. Berries bounced and rolled in great numbers.

By day's end, their arms were scratched raw from thorns and Jimmy's lips were stained red from the delicious juice. He no longer cared that the boys teased him about doing squaw's work. If he ignored them, they hissed less.

One afternoon when Jimmy and Old Mother were in a canyon shaded by high cliffs, a horrible scream pierced the air.

Several children and women with cradleboards came running toward them from the willows.

"A bear has killed my girl!" cried one woman.

Jimmy's heart squeezed tight. The woman was Nahanee's mother.

He swung onto Pinto Bean, who grazed nearby, then raced through the brush up the canyon. In a clearing he saw the bear. It was hunched over something red.

"*E-ya!*" Jimmy screamed, jumping down. He picked up a rock and threw it. Another, then another. "*E-ya!*" he kept screaming.

The bear lifted its head, annoyed at the interruption. When it saw Jimmy, it stood on its hind legs and roared. It was as tall as a tipi and it rocked back and forth, swiping its paws in the air. Jimmy could see its long, curved claws. Grizzly. It was the only animal the Indians feared.

Jimmy continued to pelt the great bear with stones, all the while screaming as loud as he could. Suddenly the bear turned, dropped to its four legs, and ambled along the stream.

Jimmy hurried to Nahanee. She lay facedown,

not moving. Her dress was soaked with blood. A beaded sleeve was torn away.

"Nahanee?" He was afraid to touch her. He didn't want to find out if she was dead. But when he saw her hand twitch in the sand, he carefully rolled her onto her back. Her eyes were closed, but he could hear her breathing. She was alive.

Quickly he searched for her wound and saw the hole in her side, blood seeping out. He ripped off his shirt and held it against her.

"Help!" he yelled. "Somebody help us!" But no one came. Jimmy struggled to lift her onto his horse. She was heavy and he was afraid of hurting her more. He lay her on her stomach with her feet toward the tail, then began running with one arm holding her on and his other hand pressing his bunched shirt against the wound. Pinto Bean trotted gently, as if she understood the importance of their mission.

As they rode out of the canyon, Nahanee tried to lift her head. "Mother?" She began crying. "Where's my mother?"

Jimmy didn't want to tell her everyone had run off.

"She's safe," he said.

When they approached camp, they were met

with cheers. Nahanee's mother rushed up, weeping for joy.

That night Nahanee's parents came to Washakie's tipi. After Washakie lit his pipe and prayed to the Great Spirit, the father spoke.

"Dawii is a brave boy, a good boy. He saved our daughter's life. What can we give him for this?"

Washakie nodded toward Jimmy. It was his turn to speak.

"I have one question," Jimmy said to the mother. "Why did you run away and leave Nahanee like that?"

The mother sat between Hanabi and Old Mother. She had the same soft face and beauty of her daughter. Her eyes filled with tears.

"I watched the bear knock Nahanee down and bite her side. I couldn't stop such a big bear. It would have killed me, also. Then two would be dead."

The father nodded. "Many get killed by a bear when they try to rescue someone," he said. "It is best to run while the bear eats the one."

Jimmy was horrified. "That's not how I would do things! If I ever see a bear attack someone, I will kill it, even if it means me getting eaten, too."

Washakie and Old Mother exchanged small smiles.

"You are a hero," Old Mother said proudly. "Everybody in the tribe will think of you as the brave one from now on. When you are a man you will be one of the greatest chiefs our people has ever had. You will bring peace to the Shoshoni."

Washakie began cleaning his pipe. Nahanee's parents stood. The mother looked tenderly at Jimmy.

"Nahanee will be your wife when you grow older," she said.

"I do not want a wife," Jimmy said, blushing. He liked to show off for Nahanee, but he didn't think it meant he should marry her. Then, remembering his manners and his responsibilities as a hero, he added, "Thank you anyway."

"You will change your mind some day," the mother said.

23

Another Girl

One morning before the sun had risen from behind the Tetons, two grizzlies wandered across a meadow.

Immediately Nampa and some other boys grabbed bows and arrows and leapt on their horses. Jimmy heard the commotion from his sleeping robe and jumped up. He strapped his quiver across his chest.

"Where are you going?" Old Mother asked.

"Bears."

"They will eat you alive, Dawii. You stay here."

Washakie stood in the doorway and held the flap open. "Let him go, Old Mother. Dawii is not in the cradleboard anymore."

Old Mother stepped back.

The grizzlies stood on their hind legs, growling in rage as the horses circled. Pinto Bean charged close enough to let Jimmy fire six arrows.

When the bears finally dropped to the ground, there were so many arrows bristling out that they looked like two fat porcupines. A strong odor wafted from their fur.

That evening the camp held a powwow and feast. At first the bear meat tasted bitter to Jimmy, but the longer it simmered in Old Mother's stew, thick with roots and mustard seeds, the more savory it became. Jimmy was thankful she no longer served him *yaha.*

Several singers sat around the drum, keeping time with their sticks. Washakie stood nearby, rattling a gourd and lifting his voice high above theirs. His headdress trailed down his back and his hair was braided; a silver hoop pierced each ear. His long-sleeved plaid shirt was made from cloth he'd traded for at Fort Hall. It hung to his knees and was belted at the waist with a beaded sash. Around his neck was a length of blue silk, fastened by a silver scarf slide from Germany. The chief sang with his face raised toward the night sky.

A circle of dancers surrounded a rack where the bear hides were stretched out like huge dark wings. Jimmy faced in with the others, moving clockwise, lifting his left foot high, then stepping with his right, over and over, left then right. He had learned this friendship dance months earlier, but this was the first time he joined in eagerly. This was his family now, this was home. He trilled his tongue in song.

Mozo sat in the shadows at the edge of the fire with the other elders. He laughed when he saw Jimmy, a laugh of affection. "The little *tybo* isn't so brave," he said aloud. "If a bear grabbed Dawii, he would run like the rest of us."

Old Mother sewed the holes in the smaller of the two hides and it made a wonderful new sleeping robe for Jimmy. Nampa gave him the claws to string into a necklace.

A few days later, another small band joined Washakie's. The girl who had hit Jimmy with his fishing pole was there and at first she glared at him. But when she saw how well he was treated by the others, she began to smile.

Finally she met him by the creek. "I am very sorry for hitting you that day," she said.

"I'm not."

"Is that so!"

"Yes. It was my kind of fun. By the way, girl, you are ugly as a fish." Jimmy didn't know why he felt so mean.

"Dawii." Old Mother stepped from behind a willow. Her voice was soft. "You make up with this girl. No more fights."

"No thanks. I'd rather dunk her in the river." Jimmy punched the girl's arm and smiled at her. She seemed to like his method for making up.

"Come to our tipi and play with me, Dawii."

"Your mother and that big knife of hers will turn me into *tybo* stew if I do."

"No! My parents are sad for all the trouble we caused."

After that Jimmy called her Big Fish Girl, a name she didn't mind one bit because now, like Nahanee, she blushed in his presence.

The warm days of summer were nearly over and the berries along the foothills had been gathered. Now that the hunters had finished their work, the women hurried to tan the remaining elk hides and make *ta-oh*. Soon they would be trading surplus buffalo robes and buckskins for red blankets, beads, calico, guns, and cooking utensils.

When Jimmy heard they would be trading at Salt Lake City, he became thoughtful. What if he saw his family? What if they saw him?

Jimmy worked even harder now, hauling all of Old Mother's and Hanabi's water. He led Red into the brush and returned with a *travois* loaded with wood for them. All teasing had stopped. No one called him squaw anymore.

Early one morning Jimmy helped Old Mother stretch and stake down a moose hide to dry in the sun. They heard giggling from behind a pine tree.

"Two birds watch you," Old Mother said without looking up.

Jimmy saw two dark heads duck out of sight. More giggles. Old Mother worked over the hide as if nothing were unusual.

Suddenly the two dashed for the woods. Nahanee and Big Fish Girl.

Jimmy was glad Nahanee's wound from the grizzly had completely healed, but he wasn't glad about her companion. What was Dawii going to do with *two* girls?

24

Rescue

Summer was over. Every few days another small band joined Washakie's and soon there were more than a thousand Shoshoni and at least five thousand horses grazing on the yellowing grass.

The air was cool as the tribe began traveling south, trailing for miles along a stream. Jimmy looked behind him and could not see the end of the line. Bright colors from beaded clothing and painted *parfleches* made Jimmy think of a rainbow snake winding its way home.

Soon they reached the fast-flowing *Piupa*. As they crossed, Old Mother's horse foundered. Jimmy tensed in his saddle as the mare struggled to regain her footing, toppling Old Mother into the icy water. Jimmy could see nothing of Old Mother except her hands flailing as she tried to grab the saddle.

"Old Mother!" Jimmy screamed as the horse swam for shore without her. He watched in horror.

Old Mother was swept downstream, her soggy red shawl the only thing visible. *She's going to drown!*

Jimmy spurred Pinto Bean into the current. But Pinto Bean stretched her neck above the surface, trying instead to return to shore. Jimmy kicked harder.

"Faster, faster!" he cried. As if understanding the desperation in his voice, Pinto Bean stopped resisting and let the river pull them along.

When they caught up to Old Mother, she was floating facedown, the red shawl bunched around her neck. Jimmy leaned down, grabbed her dress, and rolled her onto her back as he slid into the river with her.

He grabbed Pinto Bean's tail and with his other arm supporting Old Mother, he began kicking. Water splashed into his mouth, choking him. Jimmy couldn't yell instructions to Pinto Bean, but he didn't need to. She was already stumbling along the rocks toward shore, where ice had formed in the shade of the willows. Washakie waded out and carried his mother to the robe Hanabi hurriedly spread on the beach.

"Old Mother," Washakie said much later, when she was able to sit up, "I thought you were going to the Happy Hunting Grounds."

"Aii! A brave boy was with me." Old Mother

coughed several times. Finally she said, "I am not afraid of anything when Dawii is near."

Washakie made camp so Old Mother could get warm and recover. Hanabi pitched their large tipi in a cottonwood grove near the river, using all the hides. The fire inside warmed Old Mother and Hanabi kept a stew simmering. At sunset, a scout galloped up, calling for Washakie.

"Crow!" he cried, out of breath. They had overtaken a small group of Shoshoni and made off with some horses. Three men were dead.

Washakie gathered the war chief and warriors. It was cold. Stars shimmered like crystals of ice in the black sky, and wind fanned an outside fire.

"Follow the thieves all the way to Crow country if you have to." Washakie stood wrapped in his robe, his hair billowing behind him.

"I'm going, too!" Jimmy said. "I want to teach those Crow a lesson!"

"Dawii," Washakie said calmly. "Stay here. I need your bravery to protect our family."

Two days later, before dawn, a scout reported back to Washakie. No one had been killed, it turned out, and the missing horses were found. The Crow had only chased some Shoshoni to frighten them.

Another scare, Jimmy lamented to himself. *And a waste of energy*. He wondered if people would ever stop enjoying a fight. *Would there ever be peace?* He searched Washakie's face for an answer.

25

Homesick

When Old Mother felt strong enough to travel, they rode several days south, first over desert blackened with lava rocks, then past Fort Hall. Washakie's band crossed through a small mountain range to *Tosa-ibi*, Soda Springs, where they soaked in steaming hot pools.

Jimmy had never enjoyed a bath so much. He rolled and swam in the warm water. When he saw the others undo their braids, he did the same. It felt good to rub his scalp clean of the grease and dust. He listened to their prayers for good health, for peace, and for wisdom.

"The Great Spirit gives us everything," Washakie explained to Jimmy. "He gives us the Earth, our Mother, and she gives us these pools for healing. We must always give thanks for all things."

This made Jimmy think of the church his family attended, a weekly ritual he hated. The benches were hard, the bishop was loud, and the songs were slow. *How different the Indians are*, he thought. *Everything they do is connected to their religion. Every day they worship and praise the Great Spirit* who, Jimmy knew, was God.

While he sat on the bank to dry himself, steam rose from his reddened skin. He shook his hair dry. Silently, he echoed their prayers.

When the band neared Malad Pass, Washakie pointed to a small river.

"Titsapa," he said, meaning Bear River. "It flows into the Great Salt Lake."

Jimmy realized they were now close to his former home. He thought about his mother. He thought about Molly and his other sisters. He was surprised that he missed his father, too. Knowing that they were just a few days' ride away churned emotions inside him.

Old Mother saw his distress and rode her horse close to his.

"Dawii, are you sad?"

"I'm remembering my mother."

Her eyes filled with tears.

Jimmy gazed at the familiar mountain range in the east. He knew her fears and wanted to reassure her. "You are a wonderful mother to me," he said.

They traveled down to the *Titsapa* and camped three days while Washakie sorted through the hides and chose those to be traded.

Hanabi left baby Oddo in Old Mother's care so she could travel with her husband at a rapid pace. Washakie loaded twelve packhorses for his trip south, then instructed Jimmy, Nampa, and Ga-mu to take charge of the sixty-four ponies remaining in camp and to help protect the eight tipis.

"You will journey north, four suns," he told Jimmy. "At the head of *Tobitapa*, you will wait for my return, maybe fifteen sleeps."

Jimmy discovered how hard it was to get things going. He had wanted to leave by dawn, but it was quite another matter to pack up ten saddles and nine *travois*, then round up the horses and direct fifteen women, thirty-five children, and three elders.

When the sun was overhead, Jimmy's camp was finally on its way. They moved slowly north. Jimmy rode next to Old Mother.

"Why wouldn't Washakie let me go to the Mormon village?" he asked her. Old Mother kept her face ahead. Sagebrush spread around them for miles. Clouds boiled white in a turquoise sky.

"I was afraid the *tybo* would see a boy with green eyes and take him away from us."

Jimmy thought about this.

"Do not worry," she said, now looking at him. "Washakie said that if you are ever unhappy with us, he will give you your ponies and dress you like the brother of a chief. You will be escorted with honor back to your home."

Old Mother shifted Oddo's cradleboard from her back and hung it from the pommel on her saddle. Oddo was nearly two years old and heavy. She stroked the child's cheek with her finger.

"But I pray to the Great Spirit that you will never leave me, Dawii. It would kill me if you should ever go away."

"Old Mother, I want to stay with you forever. Honest."

The lines in her face moved up in a smile.

As the days grew shorter and the nights colder, they waited for Washakie and Hanabi to return. Jimmy caught fresh trout from the *Tobitapa*. By sundown his feet were numb in his wet moccasins, but Old Mother would have a dry pair waiting in their lodge. Always, there was a warm fire.

Jimmy appreciated her and felt a deep attachment that was mixed with love and the guilt he felt for having deserted his own mother. The more he thought about this, the more he was grateful for Old Mother.

He was never hungry. He had the finest, softest clothes he'd ever worn. His health was excellent. Two horses were his. He had friends and—Jimmy groaned at this—two girls adored him. Now Jimmy followed Old Mother's quiet habit. His first words in the morning were the same as his last words at night.

"Thank you, Great Spirit."

2 6

Sick Jimmy

On a cold, rainy afternoon, Jimmy was hunting sage chickens below camp on Bannock Creek. He whooped in happiness when he saw Washakie and Hanabi in the distance, leading ten packhorses. They had been gone twenty-two days.

The rain turned to sleet. By the time Jimmy had strung his chickens and ridden Red to camp he was chilled.

That night he coughed until dawn. No one in Washakie's large tipi slept.

"I will dig you a hole, Dawii," said Old Mother.

"No thank you."

"You need to sweat."

"I'm not in the mood," he said. He was shivering with fever and his throat was so swollen that it hurt to swallow. He kept sneezing. Jimmy knew that Indians loved to jump into an icy river after their saunas, a thought that now upset him.

"This will not hurt you."

"I'm too tired to swim. I am too cold already."

"Dawii." Washakie put his hand on Jimmy's shoulder. "You will do this now or the next sun will find you on your back forever."

Jimmy crossed his arms. "Then start digging." He wouldn't look at them. Why was it that one day he felt so hearty and the next day he was miserable?

Old Mother soon had prepared a hip-deep, round hole, on the riverbank with a fire, covered with stones, smoldering in the bottom.

"Take your clothes off, Dawii. Climb in."

"No." Jimmy didn't understand why he was suddenly embarrassed, but he was.

"You must."

Washakie unfolded a buffalo robe. "I will hold this around you. No one will see your white skin, Dawii."

Jimmy peeled off his buckskins, then eased himself into the hole. There was a place on either side of the rocks for his feet so he could squat without burning himself.

"Just like an old hen on her eggs," he grumbled.

Old Mother handed him a cup of water while Washakie held the robe over the hole.

"Pour it on the rocks."

Minutes passed.

"Are you sweating, Dawii?"

"I'm as wet as a fish. Can I get out of here?"

"Stay."

Minutes passed.

"Please, Old Mother. I'm so hot."

Suddenly she threw back the robe and, splash, came a bucket of icy water. Splash, came another. Another. And another.

Jimmy leapt out of the hole. Washakie caught him, wrapped him in the robe, and carried him back to their lodge. He laid Jimmy next to the fire, then piled three *bojono* robes on top of him. The fur warmed Jimmy quickly and soon he was sweating.

That night he slept.

2 7

Jimmy's Second Winter

Snow covered the mountain peaks. Now that Jimmy
was well, Washakie was in a hurry to move on to
their winter home.

While Hanabi, Old Mother, and the other women
began packing for the trip, Washakie opened the
flap of a smaller tipi and nodded for Jimmy to enter.

"Here, Dawii. For you."

Jimmy unfolded a *parfleche*. Inside were several
metal fishhooks, a new bridle, two pairs of under-
wear, a pouch full of peppermint drops, an auger,
and a knife of shiny steel with a stout leather handle.

Washakie had sold two of his horses and swapped
the *bojono* robes for metal pots and frying pans and
twenty-four red blankets, which Jimmy knew would
please the others because they loved bright colors.
There was also red flannel to use for the tongues of
moccasins, and many small bags of beads, all sizes

and colors, traded for Old Mother's tanned buckskins.

A brass bucket with a shiny new handle was the prized item; this the chief gave to his mother.

When Jimmy saw the thick squares of calico, he pictured his mother's dresses and felt a wave of sadness. But he quickly dismissed the feeling and instead wondered why Indians wanted to sew clothes from white people's cloth. Skins were so much more comfortable and soft. In winter there was nothing warmer.

When the sun was overhead Washakie's band passed Fort Hall and again forded the *Piupa*, now shallow and not as treacherous. Several days later they crossed the Continental Divide.

At the headwaters of *Angatipa* hunters enjoyed the last buffalo hunt until spring, killing sixteen, two for each tipi.

They continued west into a low mountain range with snow up to Jimmy's waist. Here, after trampling the drifts flat enough for their tents, the families camped under a full moon. Because the ground was too frozen to drive stakes, the tipi covers were wrapped lower around the poles, allowing the hems to be weighted with rocks. Jimmy helped Nampa and Ga-mu tether the horses to the trees to keep them from wandering off in search of grass.

After another day of cold, slow traveling, the Shoshoni descended to a dry valley and by nightfall were alongside a beautiful branch of the *Piupa* that shimmered under the moonlight. The next day Washakie led them to where the stream met a large river that one day would be named the Columbia.

Washakie's Shoshoni had finally reached their winter home.

The snow was heavy, but they were sheltered from the wind. The river was layered with ice thick enough for the children to play on. Jimmy marveled at the fish he could see below. The ice was as clear as if he were watching through a glass window. Mountain trout swam slowly back and forth and crayfish crept over rocks along the bottom.

An otter scurried after the trout, nosing them playfully, then darting off in another direction. It apparently was not hungry. Every few minutes it surfaced to breathe under a beaver den or a hole in the ice. It was slender with webbed hind feet and, Jimmy noticed with admiration, its coat was the color of dark chocolate.

"It would make a good skin for a new quiver, don't you think?" he asked Nampa.

They waited quietly, watching through the ice. The otter was busy chasing a fish, oblivious to the boys' shadows. Jimmy held a rock over his head.

The otter exhaled a huge silvery bubble of air that had been in its lungs.

"Now," Nampa said.

Jimmy heaved the rock through the ice, startling the otter. It hurried away, but Jimmy knew it hadn't had time to take another breath. It swam slower and slower.

Jimmy and Nampa slipped along the ice, following it. The otter's final breath had filled its lungs with water. It gave a few frantic kicks then sank to the sandy bottom.

Nampa pulled his ax from his belt to chop a hole in the ice. Jimmy scooped the dead animal out with a forked branch, then took it to camp. He skinned it and stretched the fur to dry. It was more than four feet long.

Old Mother skewered the meat over the fire. A few days later, she began embroidering the skin with rows of dyed porcupine quills and colored beads. When she sewed it together, Jimmy had the most elegant quiver in camp.

2 8

Winter Fun

Since this winter wasn't as cold as the last, Jimmy was determined to enjoy the snow as he had with his family in Utah Territory. He had a plan that he was sure no Indian had ever thought of. He was going to make a sled.

Jimmy climbed up the snowy hill bordering camp and soon had chopped enough wood. Two curved branches became runners. To these he lashed sticks crosswise.

The younger children looked at his sled with curiosity. Jimmy was so proud of himself, he bowed grandly. Nampa and Ga-mu laughed.

"Well, well," Mozo said to no one in particular. "What will the white man think of next?"

"Yes," agreed Nampa. He stood with the others, observing Jimmy's invention. Frost puffed in front of his mouth when he laughed.

Jimmy hiked up the hill, rested a moment to catch his breath, then pushed off.

"Whooopi!" Down he bounced, snow flying in his face. Children chased him, slipping and sliding, begging for a ride.

"Let's go together," he called to Nampa and Ga-mu. At the crest of the hill, Jimmy folded his furry moccasins under him and waited for the boys to climb on back. Halfway down, Nampa flipped off into a drift. But Ga-mu made it all the way down, yelling with the thrill, his pompadour coated with snow.

The next ride, five got on. The trail was so slick they shot down the hill like an arrow, tumbling into the snow at the bottom. Soon two other toboggans were made and the boys raced each other. Jimmy was pleased that he'd finally taught the Indians something. Pleased, that is, until the morning he saw Big Fish Girl with Nahanee.

At first when he saw them sledding on the other side of camp, he thought they had borrowed one of his sleds. He walked over for a closer look.

The girls were having their own fun inside the rib cage of a *bojono*, the thick backbone providing a natural runner. Jimmy watched in disbelief.

"They got that idea from me," he confided to Nampa.

"Yes. And from our grandmother's grandmother."

Day after day, the children raced each other in sleds, threw snowballs, and played stickball on the ice with an inflated deer bladder. When they hunted, two elders went along to keep the boys from killing too many animals.

In quiet moments before he slept, Jimmy watched the firelight throw long shadows against the inside of the lodge. Sparks burned tiny holes in the tipi skins, and through these holes Jimmy could see stars.

The sounds of breathing, Old Mother's ruffled snore, and baby Oddo's sigh reminded him of his family in the small cottage. Night sounds here were the same as at home. Jimmy pressed his face into the fur and stifled a sob. Was his mother thinking of him now? Did his father still need him?

Before spring, the children had made hundreds of runs on sleds. Jimmy tried Nahanee's, but when it kept rolling to the side, he decided he was no longer interested in sleds and turned his attention to hunting squirrels.

One afternoon he and several boys crept through the cottonwoods bordering a river. Jimmy suddenly screamed in pain. An arrow had pierced his thigh. Poog looked horrified.

"Oh, Dawii! I'm sorry," cried Poog. "It was an accident. Please don't choke me. Are you all right?" He watched, his face pale, as Jimmy calmly broke the shaft and pushed the flint out through the bulge in his skin. Sticky blood seeped through the fringed buckskin.

"No harm done," Jimmy said. "It was an accident."

The boys stared at him. Poog was speechless. What had happened to the Dawii of fighting and kicking fame? He was becoming more like the chief every day. He was a true brother.

2 9

Spring 1856

The snows melted slowly as the sun gained strength. Woodpeckers rattled against the trees, searching for worms in the thawing bark. Wildflowers spread color over the hills like a patchwork quilt. In the meadows, blossoms from the blue camas were so plentiful it looked as if there were small lakes.

Jimmy was happy he hadn't caused any more fights and that the Indians accepted him as one of their own now. There had been no quarrels in camp. An elder had died in her sleep and one papoose was stillborn, but otherwise all was peaceful.

Washakie moved camp downriver several miles for better grass. Mountain sheep jumped along the rocks above. Everywhere Jimmy looked there were antelope, white-tailed deer, geese, and ducks.

While Jimmy hunted with Nampa, Old Mother aired out their sleeping robes. She and Hanabi laid them over anthills so the insects would carry away the winter's grease. Sunshine soaked the furs with a rich, fresh smell.

The women rinsed all the clothes and blankets in the river, then spread them over bushes to dry. Jimmy liked the way Indian women cleaned in their calm, no-fuss way. He remembered his mother's spring cleaning and the fury with which she and his sisters scrubbed walls, corners, under beds, behind furniture, and inside places Jimmy had never thought of. They were constantly at war with dirt, every hour of the day, every season of the year.

The big fish Washakie had told Jimmy about began to swim upriver. They were as huge as he had promised. After they had stopped flopping on the bank, Jimmy could lift two at a time, slippery as they were. It was like carrying his younger sisters, he thought, Annie under one arm, Rose under the other.

Jimmy learned to throw back the female fish, for they had a sour mushy taste. Washakie told him another reason.

"These fish will die out if they cannot lay their eggs."

The salmon were fat and delicious, especially after they were smoked on racks in low tents. Hanabi and Old Mother dried enough to fill several tall sacks.

By May they had moved camp downriver, then along a canyon deep and rocky, full of snow from avalanches, now hardened to ice. There was no timber. Cliffs towered above them; bighorn sheep sometimes kicked loose stones, which rattled and bounced to the bottom. Eagles soared overhead.

"They keep watch for us," Old Mother said. "They tell their friends, the animals, we are coming and we will need them. This way the animals won't fear us."

Now they headed up a steep ravine, over a narrow switchback trail near the area where white men would soon build the mining town of Virginia City. On the crest they could see to the other side where a lush pine forest spread down to a green prairie. To the north, a fork of the Big Hole River ran through a deep gorge. They camped for weeks along a sandy beach.

Pronghorn antelope grazed on the surrounding sagebrush, often leaping playfully and showing off their white bellies. Jimmy and Washakie hunted every day so Old Mother could make *ta-oh*.

Jimmy strung the long, curved bear claws that Nampa had given to him onto a strand of twisted sinew. The necklace rattled against his chest as he walked to Nahanee's tipi. He wanted to remind her how brave he was around bears. He scratched politely on the tipi's closed flap, then waited for a voice to invite him in.

He scratched a second time. When no one answered, Jimmy turned to leave. As he did, he noticed Big Fish Girl. She stood by her mother in front of another tipi. They were not smiling. Big Fish Girl was eyeing Jimmy's necklace as she had his fishing pole.

Jimmy hurried toward his lodge as if he'd suddenly forgotten something. He knew it would be safer to wrestle a grizzly than it would be to make Big Fish Girl mad again.

30

Indian Funeral

One cool, sunny day a group of boys played battle games on their ponies, firing arrows into the air and into clumps of grass. When Jimmy saw the war chief's son crumble to the ground, he knew the playing had gotten out of hand.

The boy had an arrow in his neck and blood poured from his mouth. He was dead.

What crying followed! For five days every woman, man, and child wept in sympathy. It was a grave loss, not only for the war chief, but for the entire tribe. At first, Jimmy hid in the woods, trying to remove himself from the noise. But when he returned to camp he found it wasn't the crying that bothered him. It was the sorrow behind it.

He had liked the boy. A dull pain throbbed inside him, the exact pain he had felt when his sister Olivia died. Jimmy hadn't known what to do

with the pain then and he didn't know what to do
with it now.

The boy's mother cut off her braids and stabbed
her thighs with a flint. She slashed her arms and
pressed a blade against the last joint of her finger
until the tip was cut off. Blood soaked her buckskin
dress.

Three horses were killed to bury with the boy
so he could ride to the Happy Hunting Grounds.
His body lay on a raised pallet in the center of camp
where everyone filed by, placing a hand on his head.

"I am sorry you are leaving us," each said.

The war chief carried the body of his son to a
cliff and lay him in a crevice, covering him with a
bojono robe. Nearby, he placed a bow and arrows,
an ax, a skillet, and a pouch of *ta-oh*. The father
then closed the opening with rocks. On the beach
below, hunters were burying the three horses.

For the next five days, Jimmy tried to shut his
ears to the most heartbreaking sound he'd ever heard:
a mother weeping for a lost child. Not since Olivia's
death had he heard such a wail.

Jimmy was awed by this powerful feeling a mother
had for her son. In the evening while he lay watching
the fire, he pictured his mother at the kitchen window, looking out. Was she hoping Jimmy would ride

into the yard any minute? Did she expect him ever
to return?

Two weeks later, Washakie's band followed the Big
Hole River until it met Beaver Head River and
became the mighty Jefferson. The boys fished under
warm, blue skies.

Bojono were plenty but still thin from winter, so
they grazed peaceably nearby. Jimmy was realizing
he didn't need to kill for sport.

Prairie grasses ruffled in the wind around the
legs of the horses. Jimmy tamed two colts for Old
Mother, four for Washakie.

They broke camp and traveled northeast for a
week to the north fork of the Madison River, bordering what would one day become Yellowstone Na-
tional Park. Jimmy was fascinated by the geysers
and the boiling color pots. Great herds of elk and
antelope wandered as far as he could see. There
were too many *bojono* to count.

One morning several women with their children
rode near a stream to gather cattail down. A girl
about three years old sat atop a pony, tied securely
within the saddle's high pommel and cantle. A hiss
from the brush drew the mother's attention, but not
before the pony reared up. A rattlesnake launched

itself at the horse, which whinnied in panic and began running, the child still strapped to its back.

As it ran toward the prairie, a cluster of *bojono* sniffed the air, heads raised. Dust rose beneath their hooves as they, too, began running. The pony raced them. As it drew alongside, the herd shrank back to make room. The pony moved into the gap and was soon lost to sight as the others closed around it.

Mozo was leading Jimmy, Nampa, and Ga-mu on a hunt when they heard the stampede and tried to head it off. The *bojono* were so close Jimmy could feel the wind from their running and he could see the whites of their frightened eyes. The ground thundered under their hooves, drowning out the screams of the mother and her friends. They could see the little girl's braids flying out from the sides of her face as she bounced away.

There was nothing Jimmy could do to help. He knew the pony wouldn't be able to keep up. With a heavy heart, he watched the girl disappear, so many shaggy backs spreading like a shadow over her and the horse.

Ten minutes later the herd had passed and was now thinning into the distance. The boys rode toward the women and Mozo led the distraught mother away to keep her from seeing what had happened to her daughter.

This time, Jimmy joined the days of mourning. For once, he was not embarrassed to cry in front of friends. He wept with a force that surprised him, as if his heart had split open and poured out every hidden sorrow. He cried for the little girl and for what a child's death meant to all mothers. Jimmy cried for Olivia. And he cried for the anguish his own mother must be feeling.

When he saw Old Mother with the circle of grieving women, Jimmy remembered her loss—two sons, a daughter, a husband—and his heart felt the deepest ache of all.

The band journeyed ninety miles up the Madison River, where they camped for a month. *Bojono* were now fat enough to hunt and the cycle of making *ta-oh* and new robes began again.

As the moon waxed full, they returned to their summer campground at Henry's Lake. Jimmy fished under sunny skies and billowy white clouds.

3 1

War

Scouts rode up to Washakie as he and Jimmy fished on the shore. Crow were close, moving closer, they warned.

"We are not giving up our sacred hunting grounds because of cowards and thieves," Washakie said. He looked up to the sky, pale blue with wisps of clouds. Jimmy knew he was praying.

The next morning, the younger boys and some elders drove the surplus horses south to the *Piupa* for safety. Several women with *travois* followed so they could set up a guard camp.

Day by day, smaller bands of Shoshoni joined Washakie's at Henry's Lake. Soon hundreds of tipis were clustered in the grassy valley. Smoke rose from the cooking fires to drift in the breeze. Dogs wandered among the lodges looking for scraps. Adult laughter and the uproar of children reminded Jimmy of happy times. He didn't want to think about the reason so many were gathered.

At night, Washakie held a council in his big tipi. Before he passed his pipe, he asked the Great Spirit for wisdom and for courage.

"We have run scared from the Crow for too long. It's time we fight for our territory. We will teach them to leave us alone."

He ended with more prayer, then led the others outside to join the circle of dancers. Drummers sang with the beat of their sticks. Sparks from the bonfire sprayed up into the night.

By dawn, there were still dancers. Scouts reported to Washakie, who sat alone in his lodge. A thousand Crow were camped over the ridge.

"If there are ten thousand, we will claim our hunting grounds," the chief said.

Warriors painted black under their eyes, on cheeks and foreheads. Jimmy thought they looked fierce, but he also knew the charcoal would keep the sun's glare from blinding them. They were naked except for breechcloths and moccasins.

Their horses waited at the edge of camp, restrained by boys who yearned to be the ones racing into battle. The flanks and necks of the horses were painted with coup marks and other symbols identifying their owners. Upside-down hoof marks referred to successful raids, black teardrops meant the rider was in mourning, and handprints meant he had killed an enemy in hand-to-hand combat. Most had feathers tied into their manes; scalp locks dangled from some.

Three broad columns were forming as Washakie mounted. There were too many horses for Jimmy to count, all of them snuffing with impatience and decorated with honors.

Washakie rode forward, then turned to face the warriors. His double-tailed headdress ruffled in the wind, the many feathers signifying his successes in battle. A shield the size of a small plate was tied to his left arm. It wouldn't deflect bullets, but Washakie believed it would protect him spiritually. He gazed toward the heavens, then after a moment reined his horse around, lifted his lance, and gave a cry.

The earth shook with galloping hooves, dust clouded the air. Shouts and shrill war cries sent a chill through Jimmy. Chants from the women left behind filled him with dread. *They are mourning already*, he thought. A coil of fear turned in his stomach.

Jimmy watched as the warriors rode up the hill and stopped. They formed their lines high along the ridge. From a distance, the riders looked like bristles on a hairbrush.

Then the lines rolled from sight into the other valley. He knew Old Mother would forbid him to follow but she was in her tipi with Hanabi, who was expecting another baby any day now. Jimmy decided to run.

Several boys were already on their ponies when he reached Pinto Bean. Without speaking, they acknowledged one another by forming a line and running their horses in unison. Before they approached the crest of the hill, they dismounted and crept through the sagebrush, then lay still on their stomachs. Jimmy wondered if the others were as distressed as he was.

Below them stretched a lush valley once peaceful with grazing deer and *bojono*. Now it was crowded with horsemen fighting horsemen. Yells and trills pierced the air. Jimmy could see Washakie on his palomino, his crown of feathers flowing down his back and over the side of his saddle. He was shouting instructions to his warriors.

The Crow were also naked from the waist up, with white painted over one shoulder and around an arm. Like the Shoshoni, they wore eagle feathers in their hair. Their horses were decorated as grandly as Washakie's.

Several riderless horses raced back and forth in panic. As more bodies fell to the ground, Jimmy watched in horror. Men were dying right before his eyes and he could do nothing to stop it. A deep sorrow overwhelmed him. He buried his head in his arms.

Jimmy couldn't understand why Indians would fight each other. *If only they could be friends instead of enemies*, he thought.

When the sun reached overhead, fresh horses from camp were led to the edge of the battlefield by some older boys. Jimmy looked at the boys with envy, wishing he could be so important. He wondered how the men could ride and yell all day without water or rest. Or go a whole day without eating, something Jimmy had never done.

Near sunset, the Crows began retreating into the thick timber to the east. Dozens of stray horses wandered among the bodies. *There will be many widows*, Jimmy thought with sadness.

3 2

Scalping

There was little sleep that night. In the darkness, the wounded Shoshoni returned. There were more than three hundred of them. Jimmy followed Old Mother, helping where they could. Many did not survive the sunrise.

Jimmy nearly fainted when he saw what had happened to Nampa's brother. His nose had been shot off and one eye gouged out. But to Jimmy's amazement, One Eye—as he now would be called—smiled at him and, taking Jimmy's hand, said, "The Great Spirit has let me live."

Washakie returned leading dozens of Crow horses. His right elbow was caked with dried blood. He nodded to Mozo, who now rode with other elders onto the silent battlefield. They would guard the bodies from wolves and magpies.

By firelight Jimmy could see the piles of booty: many Crow guns, bows and arrows, saddles, and blankets. Drums beat in the darkness, singers called to the heavens. The uninjured warriors dressed themselves in their finest shirts and leggings, feathers and beads, and danced.

When the eastern sky lit with dawn, the women and children whose men had not returned made the dreaded journey over the ridge and onto the battlefield. Family friends accompanied them for comfort. When they saw all the dead, a cry rose to the wind. Jimmy's throat hurt as he tried not to cry with them. He was afraid that if he started, he wouldn't be able to stop.

The women and children wandered among the bodies, looking for loved ones. Mothers searched for their sons. Voices pleaded for fathers to wake up. A stench filled the air as the sun grew hot.

Old Mother knelt over the body of a Crow. His loincloth looked like Jimmy's; the moccasins were plain with a silver button by the ankle. Aside from the angry stripes on his cheeks, he looked as though he might have been one of Jimmy's friends. When Old Mother laced her fingers in the boy's hair, Jimmy started to back away. A knife in her other hand glistened in the sunlight as she sliced through the top of the Crow's forehead.

Jimmy reeled toward the forest. He ran and ran. *How could Old Mother do such a thing?*

From the shade of a pine, he looked back onto the battlefield. The women scalped every Crow, then left the remains for the buzzards.

Washakie's men carried their dead to a deep arroyo and covered them with rocks and dirt. The chief raised his arms to the sky and wailed. Mozo sat with a drum between his knees. With a long stick, he pounded a slow rhythm, the rhythm of a heartbeat.

3 3

Fall

Jimmy and Nampa walked near the lake where the captured horses grazed. They counted two hundred and fifty. The scouts gave Washakie more figures: forty-nine Shoshoni were killed, nearly three hundred wounded. There were one hundred and three dead Crow warriors.

They camped at Henry's Lake another three weeks so the injured could recover. Clouds of mosquitos swarmed among the wounded, biting raw skin. To discourage the insects, the women kept fires smoking with wet sagebrush day and night. They made salves from mint and cedar leaves.

By the time they could travel, the air was cold and the aspen and cottonwoods were turning to golds and yellows. Snow dusted the hills and iced the horns of the Tetons.

They divided into small bands again. Now there were many widows, so each hunter had to bring down more game to share with them. Much work was needed before they'd be ready to trade at the Great Salt Lake.

Hanabi and Old Mother toiled harder than ever, stretching and scraping hides, and smoking beef strips for *ta-oh*. Hanabi had a new papoose on her back. Nannaggai, a boy, was born three days after the battle.

They were so heavily loaded that travel was slow. Sixteen horses were packed with buckskins and *bo-jono* robes, nine were packed with *ta-oh*. At the divide, Washakie told Jimmy to stay with the others and watch the horses until his return.

Jimmy didn't like this arrangement. He wanted to see his village again; most of all, he wanted to see his mother. The horror of the scalping had not lessened his love for Old Mother, but it had deepened his yearnings for home.

Jimmy thought about this new feeling while Washakie traveled to Salt Lake City. He and Mozo were busy looking after the camp, elders, women, children and the wounded. There was much water to haul and wood to gather. The horses needed to be moved to new grass every other day. The more Jimmy thought about his family, the more he helped Hanabi and Old Mother.

After Washakie had been gone three days, Jimmy

and Nampa moved camp downstream to a wide beach that spread into sandhills. The sage chickens were plentiful here and the wounded Indians could reach the water more easily.

Jimmy was happy that fighting days were over.

Wounded

One frosty morning while Washakie was away, Jimmy heard a growl as he carried Old Mother's brass bucket up from the stream. Dust flew from behind a tipi, and before he knew it, he felt teeth bite into his leg.

It was Poog's dog.

"Blasted animal!" Jimmy kicked the dog, spilling water into the sand.

Out of the corner of his eye he saw Poog's mother lumbering toward him, lasso in hand. Suddenly, her rope landed around Jimmy's neck. She jerked him off his feet and dragged him back to her tipi. The bucket rattled down the hill. Her daughter was waiting with more rope. She tied Jimmy's hands and feet behind him while the woman held her knife over his eyes.

"Tonight, I serve *tybo* stew."

One Eye had been resting nearby. With amazing

strength he leapt into the tipi and twisted the woman's arms behind her. The knife fell into the fire ring. Jimmy could hear the cry of a child running for help.

In a wink, Old Mother was there. She slashed Jimmy's bindings, then held her own knife up to the woman, a hiss on her breath.

"Outside," Old Mother ordered.

A crowd gathered. Poog watched from a safe distance. The women eyed each other with a ferocity Jimmy had never seen.

"Stop," Poog pleaded.

Three elders stepped in and forced the mothers away from one another.

"My little son's leg was nearly bit off. Look." In the scuffle, everyone had forgotten Jimmy. He lay in the sand, blood pooling under him. The last thing he remembered was seeing the white of his thigh bone.

When Jimmy woke, the medicine man was standing over him. He passed a large fan made of eagle feathers over the leg. A poultice was tied to the wound.

By nightfall, Jimmy was shivering with fever. His leg was swollen pink. The medicine man told Old Mother to give Jimmy sips of water as often as possible. He came every few hours to change the poultice.

"You will be walking soon," Old Mother told him.

Jimmy didn't tell her his leg hurt worse by the minute. He pretended to sleep.

The next morning, Poog's tipi had been moved across the river. Nearby lay One Eye, alone on a muddy robe. His family was traveling with Washakie. He had no strength to erect his own lodge. Jimmy asked Old Mother to bring the man to their tent.

"He smells bad."

"He saved my life, Old Mother."

One Eye was too weak to walk, so Old Mother helped him onto a clean hide and dragged him into their tent.

Jimmy's stomach rose in his throat when he looked closely at his rescuer. A scabby hole was where his nose should have been. But worse was the hole in his side. The Crow arrow had narrowly missed One Eye's heart.

Old Mother went to work immediately, cleaning the wound with her sage tea. Her fist could almost fit inside the hole. The medicine man didn't help because he was busy tending the other injured.

As buffalo chips and firewood became scarce around camp, they moved south through the sandhills to a large stream they called *Tonobipa*, near piles of lava rocks.

Traveling was agony for the wounded. It had taken all day for them to reach *Tonobipa*, just five miles away. One Eye lay on a stretcher behind Old Mother's horse. Jimmy rode Pinto Bean with great difficulty. Sometimes it was less painful for him to hobble along on the crutches he made from oak branches.

By sundown, Jimmy's leg hurt so much he couldn't stand. He lay on the riverbank to drink while Old Mother hoisted the tipi herself and unpacked sixteen horses.

He was afraid to tell her he felt worse.

When she saw his face, she yelled for the medicine man. He unwrapped Jimmy's poultice. The wound was full of dark green pus.

"We must cut the leg off," the medicine man said.

3 5

Bad Medicine

"Go away! You're no medicine man!" Jimmy yelled.

"Dawii, quiet," Old Mother tried to soothe. But she began weeping so loud that several women rushed into the tipi to comfort her. When the medicine man stood, she begged him not to leave.

"My little son is out of his head with pain. He doesn't know what he is saying."

"He knows. I would be happy if the little white devil dies. He thinks he's an Indian." The man wore a hat made from the furry skull of a buffalo. The horns cast sharp shadows against the sides of the lodge.

"You'll be sorry!" Jimmy sat up. "When Washakie comes back, I'll have him cut *your* leg off. Get out now before I kick you with my good foot."

When the man stormed off, Old Mother held her face in her hands. "You are going to die now," she wept. "You have run off the medicine man."

"He's *bad* medicine, Old Mother. I didn't want to worry you, but I've felt worse, not better, since he's been around."

The air grew cooler each day. Finally it was time to break camp and head south to meet Washakie. Jimmy was too fevered to move, so five tipis remained behind with him. Mozo sat near the fire to keep Jimmy company.

Ga-mu and Nampa scouted. When they saw Washakie and the others on the horizon, they raced toward him.

"Bad medicine almost killed Dawii. Hurry!"

Without a word, Washakie leaned into a gallop. Ga-mu followed. They rode all night and half the next day with only a few stops to water their horses. When they passed another band, Washakie asked the medicine man to come to *Tonobipa*.

When he examined Jimmy, he shook his head.

"This boy would have been dead two days ago if your medicine man had his way. This sore is full of poison from the riverweed." He wrapped soft buckskin around Jimmy's leg. "He may never walk again."

Washakie opened the tipi flap. Cold air rushed in. Snow was beginning to fall.

"Bring this medicine man to me. He must be punished."

"I want to kill you," Washakie told the old man when he arrived at camp. "I should tie you to the tail of a wild horse and let it kick you across the prairie until there is not enough meat left on your bones for the wolves. But that would be too kind."

Washakie stood taller than the man. Anger flashed in the chief's eyes.

"Instead, you are to leave here. No woman, no warrior, no elder, no child of the Shoshoni tribe will ever look at you again." Snow swirled around the flap as Washakie opened it.

"I have spoken. Now go."

At the new medicine man's instruction, Ga-mu gathered heart-leaf arnica from the forest. The salve Old Mother made from this plant would counter the infection. Every two hours through the night she bathed the wound with warm sage tea. She rubbed cool water on Jimmy's forehead to try to break his fever. The hours were long and dark, but by dawn his fever was gone. He slept all day and the next night.

By the second morning, he felt better. When Washakie said they must travel south, Jimmy tried to climb on Pinto Bean but his leg wouldn't move.

"Here, Dawii." Washakie led him to Old Mother's best horse. "Wait here."

Washakie and Nampa went to work. They took

two tipi poles and lashed them to the side of Old Mother's saddle, then wove rope between the poles to form a stretcher that would drag behind the horse. Onto this they piled four *bojono* robes. Jimmy climbed aboard for the most luxurious ride of his life.

3 6

Mozo

From his stretcher, Jimmy watched the sky and the Shoshoni trailing behind. The robes were soft around him and warm. Only his face felt the cold autumn air. The poles scraping along the ground reminded him of Mozo drawing stories with a stick in the dirt.

During those days of fever, Mozo had sat on a robe in the back of the tipi, the warmest spot and the place of honor. He had talked about the old ways and about the first white men he had seen, two white chiefs called Lewis and Clark. They came with thirty-five men and a Shoshone girl named Sacajawea, who helped the explorers find their way west to the great waters.

"Those men were honest," Mozo had said. "They were good men. We sold them twenty-nine horses. For ten suns I traveled with them. I gave them fish I caught and they gave me shirts. At the time, your brother Washakie was a boy of six winters."

Sacajawea was also young, about fifteen winters, Mozo said. She was married to a French fur trapper and along the whole journey she carried her infant son on her back.

"Sacajawea helped the white chiefs understand us. But she couldn't stop what was to be. The white chiefs said their mission was one of peace, but they gave many guns to the Indians. This is something I don't understand. Now these guns are used in war.

"I am not against the *tybo*," Mozo continued. "But they do not respect Mother Earth. Before they came, the elk and fish were plenty. The streams were clear. *Bojono* were more than you've ever seen, Dawii. More than grains of sand on the shore.

"We have been told that far toward the sunrise, *tybo* shoot our Brother *Bojono* for fun. They take the skins but leave the meat for the buzzards."

Jimmy had been uncomfortable listening to Mozo's tales. If Old Mother hadn't been sitting in the shadows, silent in agreement, Jimmy might have wondered how true these stories were. The more he heard about his people, the less he wanted to return to them. He had heard white men claim, "The only good Indian is a dead Indian." It was small comfort to know his father would never say such a thing.

The gentle rocking in his stretcher made Jimmy feel calm. He was warm and sleepy nestled in the

162

robes. Old Mother often looked back at him and smiled. Low gray clouds hid the sun all day, making a soft backdrop for the V's of flying geese.

Jimmy thought about his long hours in the tipi with Mozo. He remembered how the firelight made the old man's face look golden. Sometimes the elder would close his eyes and be silent. Just when Jimmy thought Mozo must be asleep, he would begin speaking again.

"There were *tybo* who carried mail to California from the Great Salt Lake. They would steal horses from settlers, then hide them with us for two moons, though we didn't realize they were stolen. When the *tybo* came back for these horses, they always gave us red blankets.

"But once, the settlers followed the tracks. When they saw their horses with ours, they started shooting. No chance for us to explain.

"I had been gone on a hunt, and when I returned I found these *tybo* had killed my eldest son and six other warriors."

The story continued. Mozo waited eight days. In the middle of a storm, he and some others stampeded a wagon train and took twenty-two horses. When Mozo reached camp, Washakie came to hear his story.

" 'I do not blame you, Mozo,' Washakie said.

'This is a sad thing, fighting with *tybo*. Stay away from their road and stay away from them. I forbid fighting. We must try to have peace with these new people.' "

Mozo had paused again. Jimmy saw that his eyes were closed. After breathing deeply, the elder continued.

"Once ten wagons with white tops camped near us." Mozo had drawn a circle in the dirt floor with his stick and marked the positions of the wagons and then another circle where the tipis had been. "The *tybo* children were sick all night with coughs so loud it sounded like dogs barking. Soon, the Indian children coughed and after three suns, many were dead.

"The Chief With Many Squaws is making many villages. He wants his people to live where game is plenty and rivers are full. They want us to move south to where the snakes and lizards are. They think we will be happy eating horned toads for breakfast!"

As Jimmy lay in the tipi, listening, he didn't know how to respond. He did know that the Chief With Many Squaws was Brigham Young and he knew Young's settlements were branching out beyond Salt Lake City farther into the heart of Shoshoni country.

Jimmy hadn't realized what the Indians thought

of white people and now he felt ashamed. The whites were moving in uninvited. Their ranches and their miles and miles of fences were going to block the Shoshoni trails. If Indians would stop fighting each other, maybe together the tribes could stop the *tybo*'s fences.

The only honorable thing to do, Jimmy decided, was to pledge loyalty to the Shoshoni. He was fourteen years old; soon he would be a warrior. He would live with them until his dying day.

After his ride on Old Mother's *travois*, Jimmy felt strong enough to help set up their tipi in winter camp. By the next moon, his leg was healed and he was happy to gather buffalo chips and haul wood from the abundant supply on the hillside. Most of the wounded were healthy again. Even One Eye sang to the Great Spirit in thanksgiving, for he married the beautiful sister of Nahanee.

3 7

Council

Snow was falling when Chief Pocatello—the White Plume—rode into camp with several warriors. Frost steamed from the horses' mouths and huge white flakes settled on their manes and forelocks. Smoke curled up from the big tipi where Washakie and the visitors sat.

When Jimmy tried to enter, Mozo stopped him. "Go away, Dawii."

Jimmy ran to Old Mother's tipi. Hanabi was there, nursing her baby, and both women were crying.

"What's going on?" Jimmy asked, afraid there would be another war.

They didn't answer.

The powwow went on for four days. When Jimmy approached his friends or Old Mother, they became silent. He felt cold. The council must be talking about him.

On the fifth day, Washakie sent for Jimmy. Jimmy

stooped under the flap and found fifteen Shoshoni sitting in a large circle around the fire. He sat cross-legged at Washakie's right.

For a long while, the only sound was the crackle of flames in the warm tent. Finally Chief Pocatello spoke.

"How many winters are you, Dawii?"

"Fourteen and a half, sir."

"Were you captured or did you run away from your people?"

"I ran away. Ga-mu and Nampa gave me a pony so I could ride with them to their camp." Jimmy was so nervous he could have talked all day. Should he explain that he had thought his visit would be for just a day or two?

Pocatello sat quietly. His face didn't give away his thoughts. Jimmy was worried about what the notorious chief might be planning.

"You may go now," White Plume said finally.

Jimmy ran back to his tipi, where Old Mother and Hanabi asked him question after question.

That night, another council met in Washakie's big tipi. Pocatello sat opposite Jimmy.

"How long have you lived with the Shoshoni?" the chief asked.

"This is my third winter."

"Have you been mistreated?"

Jimmy thought about that. He decided not to tell on Poog and Big Fish Girl or their mothers. "I've been treated very well."

"Why did you run away from your people?"

Jimmy hesitated. "I was mad at my father. He wouldn't let me have a horse."

The chiefs said nothing; their silence filled Jimmy with shame. A log burning in the ring collapsed into the coals with a hiss.

Finally Washakie spoke. His eyes were cast down. "Dawii, would you rather live with Indian people or white people?"

Jimmy knew the answer, but still there was a catch in his throat.

"Indians," he said proudly.

The council broke up late that evening. Jimmy again asked Washakie what was going on.

"We will know at sunrise."

Jimmy lay awake all night.

38

No More War

The next morning, Jimmy hurried to the big tipi. He hadn't touched Old Mother's breakfast. More Shoshoni crowded in.

Washakie spoke.

"Twelve suns ago, White Plume's Indians were in the big *tybo* village. They were asked if they had seen the white boy who was stolen from them.

"They said the boy is called Jimmy Spoon and his family wants him back. There will be a war and many Indians will die if he is not returned. Dawii's father is raising up a big army on the next moon."

The council was silent. Jimmy's mind raced with questions. Why had his father waited until now to look for him?

Nothing made sense. He told all this to Washakie.

"It makes no sense to me either, Dawii."

Pocatello's eyes narrowed. "You can keep this

little *tybo* if you want, but if there is a war over him, do not ask us to help you."

"As for me," a boy whispered to Nampa, "I'll take that white devil into the willows so we can have another pretty scalp to dance with."

"Not as long as I'm here, you won't," Nampa answered.

"Aii," two others said in unison. "We will stand by Dawii."

"Dawii is our brother." Ga-mu spoke, his right hand over his heart.

Jimmy saw Poog watching him. The boy's face was stony, but Jimmy thought he saw a flicker of friendliness in his eyes.

That night, there was another council. Jimmy sat in the shadows behind Washakie. Nearly an hour slipped by as the pipe was passed. No one spoke.

Finally, Washakie lay the pipe across his knees. They didn't want to fight with the white people, he said. But Dawii was his brother. He was brave and twice saved Old Mother's life. He rescued Nahanee from the bear. He listened to his elders. He had taken the feather from an eagle without hurting the bird. Dawii was an honored Shoshoni brother.

"My heart hurts to think he must go from us."

Shadows behind each man danced up the side

of the tipi. The fire snapped and hissed in the silence.

"If some Indians go to the *tybo* village, they can find out what is really happening," Washakie said.

"Who will go?" asked Mozo.

"The boy should go." It was Pocatello. "It would be better this way."

Washakie looked at Jimmy. "What do you think about this, Dawii?"

"I'd get lost, and besides, I do not want to go. I *won't* go."

"There must be no war, Dawii. There must be peace."

Yes, Jimmy thought. He squeezed his eyes shut to keep the tears back.

Washakie asked each man in the circle what he thought. One by one they said the same thing.

"The boy should go. It is the best that can be done."

Ten minutes passed. The lodge was warm from the fire. Smoke drifted up to the small opening where stars sparkled against a black sky. Jimmy was afraid to look at the faces. Finally Washakie spoke.

"The decision is yours, Dawii."

39

"Un-voin-ahee"

Jimmy rode Red into the woods. Snow drifted through the branches, settling on the fur draped over his shoulders. He was cold and he was crying. Never before had he felt so lonely.

He didn't want to leave his Shoshoni family. He didn't want to wear hard shoes or buttoned collars or be stuck inside a gloomy store all day. Would he ever see Nahanee again?

Most of all, what would happen to Old Mother? Jimmy felt worse when he remembered her lost children and that now she would lose him, too.

He was bothered by so many questions. What would his father do to him? If he wouldn't let him return to the Shoshoni, would he have to run away again? And what then? Jimmy didn't want to ever see another battle.

Jimmy wanted peace.

Old Mother wept when she heard Jimmy's decision. Hanabi buried her face in her hands. They begged Washakie to send someone else to the Mormon village.

Sadness showed in the chief's eyes. "I will send Nampa and Ga-mu with him. They will show Dawii the way.

"Go home, tell your father the truth. If you want to come back to us, come. We will be happy if you live with us forever."

"I'll come back. I will go tell them I'm all right. Then I will come back. Soon."

Washakie stood in front of the tipi, his arms folded inside his robe. Tears welled in his eyes.

Jimmy was uncomfortable with the chief's silence. "Will you miss me?" He felt stupid for asking, but he didn't want the conversation to end.

When Washakie looked at Jimmy, a tear spilled out of one eye and slid down his wrinkled cheek.

"When a *tybo* is happy or sad, he feels it in his head and his tongue speaks. An Indian feels these things in his heart, and the heart has no tongue."

Six days later, Jimmy was ready to leave. Hanabi, Old Mother, and several women had spent hours sewing clothes fit for the brother of a chief. The young boys gave Jimmy enough arrows to fill three quivers. Jimmy was showered with so many gifts, he needed an extra horse to help carry the fifteen buckskins, ten pairs of beaded moccasins, and the seven *bojono* robes. Washakie gave Jimmy a Crow pony to accompany Red and Pinto Bean.

An unsmiling Poog handed him an eagle feather. *"Un-voin-ahee,"* Poog said. *We'll see you again.*

Jimmy had learned that Shoshoni didn't say good-bye to friends. He accepted the peace offering, a quiet joy soaring inside him.

But it was the sight of Nahanee that most lifted his heart and filled him with determination. He *would* return. Vermilion was painted down the part in her hair and on her cheeks, symbolizing peace. As she stood by her mother in the morning sunlight, Jimmy placed the bear claw necklace over her head. She smiled, knowing he planned to return to her.

A mile out of camp, Jimmy looked back. His feather ruffled at the side of his head. He could see Old Mother's lodge and he knew she was inside. The wind whisked smoke from her fire up to a cold, blue sky.

Even from this distance, he could tell the horse-man on the hill was Washakie. Jimmy raised his arm in salute, then turned to the trail where Nampa and Ga-mu waited.

Reunion

Henry Spoon rolled back the awnings to let in the morning light, then studied the window display. Several mannequins were dressed in the latest style of men's wool caps and waistcoats, women's cloaks, muffs, and winter bonnets.

Boughs of pine and holly trimmed the front doors. A small sign clipped to a wreath had a discreet reminder for customers: "Thirty-seven days until Christmas."

As Henry swept the night's dusting of snow from the sidewalk, he heard a commotion down the street. He folded his hands over the top of the broom and listened.

Three girls were running toward him, pigtails flying and unlaced boots flapping.

"Father, Father!" they cried through the frosty air.

Emma, Frances, and Annie were racing each

other and yelling with excitement, each one wanting to be the first to tell the news.

Henry heard the words "Indian" and "Jimmy." He leaned the broom against the adobe storefront just in time to catch five-year-old Annie in his arms.

". . . and his face is dirty. Are you gonna wup him like you promised, Father?" She turned to her sisters to stick out her tongue. "I got here first."

"He's home, Father," Emma said, out of breath. "Mama was scared that an Indian was coming into the yard . . ."

"He smells," Annie interrupted.

". . . but when Mama saw his eyes, she dropped the bread pan and said, 'Run get your pa.' "

Henry started walking. Annie wiggled from his arms to run alongside.

"Hurry, Father," Frances pleaded, her long strides pressing into the snowy street.

"What're you gonna do, Father?" asked Emma.

Henry Spoon's throat was too tight to answer. The angry words he'd rehearsed for this hour suddenly dissolved. He was surprised to feel tears filling his eyes.

"You girls run ahead," he said softly. "Tell your mother I'm coming."

Epilogue

For three and a half years Jimmy helped his father run Spoon's Fancy Store in Salt Lake City. When he turned eighteen, he signed on as a Pony Express rider, where he met up with more Indians, some friendly, some not. He also began searching for Nahanee.

But that's another story.

Glossary of Shoshoni Words

Angatipa—Rock Creek, Washington

Bannock—"hair in backward motion," referring to men's pompadour; Idaho tribe

bojono—buffalo

Dawii—young brother

deeba—pine nuts

Ga-mu—rabbit

Gosiutes—"dust people"; a Shoshoni-speaking tribe from the southwest area of Utah's Great Salt Lake

iki—right here

kinnikinnick—(origin, Algonquian) tobacco, often made from willow bark, sumac leaves, bearberry leaves

Koheets—A creek near the Idaho–Utah border

Mozo—whisker

Nampa—moccasin

Paitapa—Jefferson River, Montana

parfleche—(origin, French) large rawhide pouch

shaped like an envelope, sometimes brightly painted or decorated with beads and porcupine quills

Piupa—Snake River

Pocatello—White Plume

Sogwobipa—Missouri River

ta-oh—jerky

Teewinot—many pinnacles (the Tetons)

Titsapa—Bear River, a fresh river that flows south into the Great Salt Lake

Tobitapa—Portneuf River, Idaho

Tonobipa—a creek near Blackfoot, Idaho

Tosa-ibi—Soda Springs, Idaho

travois—(origin, French) stretcher to carry people or belongings, made from two tipi poles secured on each side of a horse; it drags along the ground

tybo—white person

un-voin-ahee—we'll see you again

waazip—lost

Washakie—rawhide rattle

yaha—yellow-bellied marmot

Bibliography

America's Fascinating Indian Heritage. Pleasantville, N.Y.: The Reader's Digest Association, 1978.

Boren, Marjorie D., and Boren, Robert R. *Mountain Wildflowers of Idaho.* Boise, Idaho: Sawtooth Publishing Company, 1989.

Capps, Benjamin. *The Great Chiefs.* Alexandria, Va.: Time-Life Books, 1975.

Capps, Benjamin. *The Indians.* Alexandria, Va.: Time-Life Books, 1973.

Conley, Cort. *Idaho for the Curious.* Cambridge, Idaho: Backeddy Books, 1982.

Deseret News. Salt Lake City, Utah: 1850–1856.

Drimmer, Frederick, ed. *Captured by the Indians: Fifteen Firsthand Accounts, 1750–1870.* Mineola, N.Y.: Dover Publications, 1961.

Freedman, Russell. *Buffalo Hunt.* New York, N.Y.: Holiday House, 1988.

Freedman, Russell. *Indian Chiefs.* New York, N.Y.: Holiday House, 1987.

Madsen, Brigham D. *Chief Pocatello: "The White Plume."* Salt Lake City, Utah: University of Utah Press, 1986.

Madsen, Brigham D. *The Northern Shoshoni.* Caldwell, Idaho: Caxton Printers, 1980.

Mails, Thomas E. *Dog Soldiers, Bear Men and Buffalo Women*. Englewood Cliffs, N.J.: Prentice-Hall, 1973.

Mails, Thomas E. *The Mystic Warriors of the Plains*. New York, N.Y.: Doubleday, 1972.

Schultz, James Willard. *Sinopah, the Indian Boy*. Bozeman, Mont.: Museum of the Rockies, Montana State University, 1984.

Sho-Ban News. Fort Hall, Idaho: 1987–1989.

Wilson, Elijah Nicholas. *Among the Shoshones*. Medford, Oreg.: Pine Cone Publishers, 1910.